Simple and Pure

MICHAEL RAHLFS

CONTENTS

CHAPTER 1

After finishing the Morning Prayer, Thomas Clarke made the Sign of the Cross and placed his worn copy of the Liturgy of the Hours on the dresser. At his feet was a plastic storage container filled with reminders of the past: awards for debate and Latin composition, pictures of friends, tokens from school trips, a large football championship ring, and many books. The world had changed considerably for the entire Clarke family over the last ten months, and today Thomas would have to choose for himself a proper response. What would command his soul?

He smiled as he glanced at the one old photo remaining on the wall. A group of laughing children stood in a clearing surrounded by tall pine trees, with the bend of a small creek in the distance. Thomas and a tall, skinny, dark-haired girl wearing large glasses were among the tanned crowd at the parish picnic. He looked down at the storage bin. Out of sight and out of mind would be the easiest course of action. Although he took the photograph down and hastily placed it in the bin, he could not bring himself to seal the lid and shove it all into the closet.

CHAPTER 1

On the nightstand next to the bed lay *The Imitation of Christ,* which he had specifically bookmarked before going to sleep the previous night. He walked over, sat on the bed, and began to read: *The quality of a man's virtue is best displayed in difficult times, and far from weakening him, such times reveal him for what he really is.*

Thomas took in a deep breath and let it out slowly. He prayed aloud, "Lord, let this be one day that is well lived."

Gathering up his book bag, he came down the stairs of a modest Chicago bungalow and entered the small, clean kitchen as his mother finished arranging Kathleen Clarke's wavy, blonde hair into a ponytail. Margaret Clarke eyed her work from a few different angles and announced that she was done. Her daughter twirled in a flash, but before the excited ten year old could get one step away, her mother calmly stated, "No running, young lady." Kathleen composed herself, smiled sheepishly, and walked to the hallway mirror to examine her hair and her new fifth-grade school uniform. She had worn a white cotton blouse with a plaid wool skirt the year before. This morning, however, the pattern colors were red and black instead of blue and black. Her mother called her back for breakfast.

Margaret gave a quick "good morning" greeting to her son and returned to the oatmeal on the stove. Thomas kissed her on the cheek and took his usual seat at the kitchen table. Kathleen joined him as the piping hot bowls were served. As he began to eat, Thomas noticed that his sister was not eating. Instead, she just sat and stared at him. She had never seen him go off to school in anything other than an official St. Titus School uniform: dark shoes, dark blue pants, a white shirt, and a blue-and-gold tie. Khaki pants and a blue button-down shirt were certainly presentable, but still they seemed strange and out of place. Margaret gently reminded her daughter that time was short, and Kathleen picked up her spoon.

After sprinkling some raisins in his oatmeal, Thomas asked, "Do you like your new uniform, Kathleen?"

She nodded her head enthusiastically and said, "I do! Very much!"

"Aren't some of your friends from St. Titus going to be in your new classroom?"

"Yes, Nora, Susan, and Mary will be in my room, and Jackie and Clare will be in the other room."

"I think you are going to like Queen of Heaven School," Thomas said reassuringly.

"I hope so. I wish you were coming, though," Kathleen confided.

He wanted to be there with her more than she would ever know, but fate had determined otherwise.

Thomas leaned in next to her and lovingly said, "Courage. Everything will be all right. Before you know it, your new classmates will be your new friends, and this school will be a lot like St. Titus was."

She nodded and smiled with the face of an angel. If Thomas said it was going to be okay, then it was going to be okay. Thomas never lied.

She asked him, "What do you think your new school will be like?"

"Well, public school certainly will be different from Catholic school," he acknowledged, "but we all have challenges to face. How you respond to them is what makes you happy or sad. I say that we decide to face the world with courage and hope. What do you say?"

"Courage and hope," Kathleen replied in agreement before finishing off her breakfast.

John Clarke had retrieved the morning paper from the doorstep and heard his children's conversation from the dining room. He came into the kitchen, put his arm around his wife's waist, and gave her a kiss. This morning, the squeeze he gave her was a little stronger and the kiss lasted a little longer than usual. Margaret looked at her husband, smiled, and then said sweetly, "Courage and hope."

The archdiocese had announced that the St. Titus Class of 2008 would be its last. The parish, the grammar school, and the high school would all be closing at the end of the school year. With them went the much-needed tuition break the pastor had given to John Clarke and his family. Business at Clarke Printing had been dropping off steadily since the middle of 2007 and was getting worse every month. Over the past spring and summer, the home furnace died, followed quickly by Margaret's car. One expense after the next was slowly draining the family's savings.

Even though John never said a word to his son about the family's finances, Thomas had worked part time at his father's print shop long enough to know that things were getting tight. In January, before St. Titus closed, Thomas insisted on going to a public high school for his senior year. His father absolutely refused, but as the economy worsened, John had to accept the dismal reality. Even with his wife working, the bills were piling up, and he could not afford to send both of his children to Catholic school in the fall.

So the hard decision was made. Kathleen would go to Queen of Heaven, which was also the family's new parish, and Thomas would try to get into the best public high school he could. His grades were stellar, and after completing a series of rigorous tests, Thomas had outperformed thousands of other applicants to receive one of the three available slots in the Advanced Placement (AP)/Honors program at West Ridge Prep. (The other two recipients were freshmen.) Luckily, the school was close to home.

Everything was going to work out; John and Margaret Clarke would make sure of that. They had no control over what happened in the world, but inside the walls of their home, by the grace of God, there would be happiness, peace, and love. Their hand had been dealt, and no matter how unfair it seemed, especially concerning Thomas, they would always have hope. Courage and hope.

Kathleen rinsed her bowl in the sink and put on a backpack loaded down with school supplies. She gave her father a hug. He bent down and said to her, "Sweetheart, I know you are going to do great today." She gave him another hug and a kiss. He stood up and commented in a serious tone, "After all, nothing ever stays the same, does it?"

She thought for a second and then replied, "Except for love and truth."

"That's my girl," her father said proudly.

Margaret grabbed her keys, kissed her husband and son, and led her daughter into a new day. Kathleen hurried out to the car and waved good-bye to Thomas. He waved back in reply and then went to clean up what was left of breakfast.

John came up to his son hesitantly and said, "Tom, I know this is going to be a tough year for you."

Thomas turned and stood up straight, facing his father eye to eye. For the first time, John noticed how much his son had grown. Thomas had always been one of the smaller boys in his class, but now he stood before his father like a grown man.

"Dad, it's just school, and West Ridge has one of the best academic reputations in the state. It can't be that much different than St. Titus. Besides, it's only going to be one school year, not even a whole calendar year," Thomas said cheerfully. He never complained once to his parents or gave any hint of disappointment with his present situation.

"That is true, but I know all your friends went to other schools, and your mom and I wish . . . uh . . . we could have . . . given you—"

As his father struggled for words, Thomas jumped in and said with a wry smile, "Dad, I pray that I may continue to have as I have now, or less; and that I may live sufficiently for what remains of my life, if the gods permit that any of it remain."

His father shook his head, amazed once again at his son's memory, and asked, "Who was that from?"

"Horace. Not bad for a pagan Roman, huh?"

John chuckled and slapped his son on the shoulder, "Tom, your mother and I appreciate what you are doing very much, and we are proud of you."

Thomas would rather die than let down his parents, to whom he owed so much. He gave his father a hug and said, "Thanks, Dad."

Locking the door behind them, father and son stepped out into a beautiful, warm late summer morning. A soaring deep blue sky was filled by the soft light of the rising sun, which gave the streaks of thin clouds a reddish-yellow tint. It reminded Thomas of Homer, the ancient Greek poet. As a light breeze blew through the trees, John wished his son good luck once more and began to walk north and east toward the print shop. Thomas turned south and west.

The chirping of a sparrow and the distant whistling of a robin were the only sounds on the empty street. In the silence and solitude, Thomas's mind could settle without distraction. The natural beauty that surrounded him was tremendously helpful. He thought as he walked, *Where there is beauty, there is truth, goodness, and life, for the nature of the good is in alliance with the nature of the beautiful. Measure and proportion manifest themselves in all areas of beauty and virtue.* The rarity of these moments made him appreciate them even more, as his mind and soul could let go of the mutable, imperfect, and finite to ponder the unchanging, the perfect, and the eternal—that which is. The rest of the day would be his attempt—and often failure—to speak and live the good, just, and true. It was only a twenty-minute walk to school, but at least he would have that time for contemplation every morning.

The most direct path to his new school, though, led right past the former St. Titus campus. It was surreal as he came upon it. Because the local public grammar school was overcrowded, the Chicago Public School system now rented the classrooms from the archdiocese. Children jumped out of cars, SUVs, and minivans and ran into the old building of elaborate brickwork and ornate masonry. Large yellow buses pulled up and unloaded their precious cargo as the traffic jammed and chaos ruled. Built in 1924 for neighborhood children who walked everywhere they went, the school entrance was overwhelmed with vehicles and people despite the best efforts of teachers and administrators trying to bring order.

Entirely detached from the commotion, Thomas remained on the opposite side of the street and watched the bustle of activity from a distance. This had been his home away from home for most of his life, but now, despite the mass of humanity, the place was dead to him. It was like being at a wake.

Again, he thought of Homer, specifically of Odysseus on his way back to Ithaca, traveling through the Kingdom of the Dead, seeing the souls of his lost loved ones and fallen comrades, and speaking to the great Achilles in Hades because Achilles had been consumed by pride. Achilles stated that he would give anything to be a slave on earth to a poor farmer than to rule the breathless dead in the underworld.

As Thomas moved on past his old school, the wise words of King Alcinous to Odysseus became more clear: "Balance is best in all things." *For there to be peace, happiness, and freedom in your soul,* Thomas reflected, *that which is of a higher nature must command that which is of a lower nature. Who does not desire peace, happiness, and freedom?*

Thomas Clarke resolved that today reason and love would command his soul, not any passion or emotion. *Better to be free in truth and alive than to be enslaved in pride and dead,* he thought to himself. He turned the corner and soon came upon the river. Through the trees in the distance stood the shimmering new campus of West Ridge Prep.

***

John came out of his office and carefully examined the weathered brick facade of his family's business. It was rather plain, but the old building did have some character. In his hand was a letter from the City of Chicago Department of Buildings informing him that the walls need to be tuck-pointed and the air circulation system's ductwork needs to be cleaned. He scratched his head. The building had been tuck-pointed two years ago, and he personally cleaned the air duct over the rear door every Monday morning.

Clarke Printing opened for business in 1957 across the street from an elevated Chicago and North Western Railway line. The grass, which grew tall during the summer, lilted downward on the slope from the railroad tracks toward the two-foot-thick by five-foot-high concrete support base. Scattered amid the grass, purple and yellow wildflowers made the scene very picturesque. That was, of course, until the massive trains roared by. Up twenty feet in the air and moving at fifty miles per hour, the freight and commuter cars produced a deafening sound and shook everything in sight.

After emigrating from Ireland to the United States in 1947 and after renting out business space for years, Patrick Clarke thought he had finally found the perfect building for his print shop. It was within walking distance from his house but still far enough away from residential areas. He had figured that no rational person would want to live that close to these railroad tracks. Single-family homes and apartment buildings did come, though. By the time John Clarke took over running the business in the early 1980s, only two other industrial buildings remained where there had once been more than twenty.

Meticulous in every aspect, Patrick Clarke had run a tight ship. Blood, sweat, and tears had been poured into getting his print company started and eventually making it successful. John had worked there his entire life, and his father had taught him well. This letter from the city did not make any sense at all.

"Hey, George, come out here for a minute, please."

Clarke Printing's oldest and only remaining full-time employee came over and read the letter his boss handed to him.

"That young laddie from the city was no more than twenty-four or twenty-five years old," George Stanton declared in a thick County Mayo brogue despite having lived in Chicago for the last forty years. "I'm thinking the idiot doesn't even know what tuck-pointing is."

"Apparently, he doesn't know much about an air duct system either." John shook his head as he read the rest of the letter. "Well, according to this, we have one month to fix things that are not broken, and then we will have to attend an administrative hearing and pay some kind of fine." The phone rang in the office.

Margaret could tell that her husband had a headache simply by the way he answered the phone, so she was happy to give him some good news. She explained that although Kathleen became apprehensive as she approached her new school, when she got out of the car, a gaggle of excited girls whom she already knew came up and welcomed her. She waved briefly to her mother and went without the slightest hesitation into her new school. "Kathleen is going to be fine," Margaret assured her husband. "We all are going to be fine."

John's wife was a woman of few words, but she was the undeniable rock of the Clarke family. He could not imagine life without her. Somehow she instinctively knew when he was getting downhearted and was always able to pick him up as she did this morning. The only person he had ever known to be more optimistic and steady than Margaret was their son. The boy never flinched. It would be a foolish endeavor for anyone to get into a battle of wills with Thomas. His son could certainly handle one year of school at West Ridge Prep. John felt much better now. His daughter had settled in, and there was no reason to doubt that Thomas's first day was going fine as well.

As he said good-bye to his wife and hung up the office phone, he looked down at the other mail on his desk and saw a letter from the Cook County assessor's office with his adjusted property taxes. The telephone rang again. The caller ID showed it was his wife's cell phone.

CHAPTER 2

Spread out on fifteen acres straddling the north branch of the Chicago River, West Ridge Preparatory Academy was massive and impressive. Thomas made his way toward the main entrance, observing a host of vehicles pull up in the excessively spacious parking lot and efficiently disperse throngs of students. This was the start of the school's fourth year, and by now, almost everything appeared to run smoothly, as originally designed.

During the 1980s, epic battles were waged in Chicago over bussing and desegregation. Back then, 40 percent of public school students were Caucasian. Now, Caucasians comprise less than 10 percent of Chicago's public school student population. There were no "white schools" anymore. As demographics and culture shifted, the problem became how to entice white families to stay in the city and send their children to public schools that were generally seen as dangerous and little more than a joke academically.

The powers that be came up with the typical solution: a massive public works program. One new school would be built in each part of the city: downtown, south, and north. Only students who tested at the highest level were to be

11

admitted. This being Chicago, though, many deals and compromises had to be made to win support for the project. The politicians received abundant, glowing press and doled out huge construction contracts to their supporters. Any adornment they desired for each of the three new schools was not denied. Minority and community activists were able to get certain students admitted regardless of their test scores, and these activists were also assured that a large number of additional jobs would be created and given to members of specific interest groups. No one questioned when the original budget of $50 million per school more than tripled.

Thomas walked up to the tinted doors and checked the slip of paper that listed his classes. An additional note obliged him to visit with the principal before his first class. After holding the door for two perplexed girls, Thomas tried to follow them inside, but a large security guard in a dark blue jacket stuck a flashlight in his chest and asked him brusquely, "Where do you think you're going?"

Taken aback, the only answer that came to him was the truth. "To school, sir."

"Through the machine first, smart guy."

A small army of private security guards and Chicago police officers stood inside every entranceway of the school. They were funneling students through metal detectors and pulling aside and patting down anyone they deemed suspicious. It looked like something out of Joliet State Prison, but Thomas calmly cleared security and entered into the spotlessly clean atrium and its new glass dome, which had been built over the summer with a $2 million state grant.

The principal's office was situated just off the south end of the atrium, and Thomas arrived early. A smartly dressed older woman sat at a desk, reviewing some papers. Behind her, a short middle-aged man in white overalls and a T-shirt was meticulously painting large, elaborate letters on a door: *Dr. Ricardo Diaz, PhD.*

Thomas gingerly walked up to the woman and said, "Good morning, ma'am. My name is Tho—"

Without looking up, she abruptly cut him off by asking harshly, "Why are you here?"

"Please excuse me, ma'am. I have a note that says I am to see Principal Diaz."

The note was snatched out of his hand and set facedown on the desk. Thomas stood patiently, waiting until the woman finished her paperwork and finally read the note that was clearly stamped *AP/Honors* at the top.

"Oh, I am terribly sorry. I did not realize who you were. I thought you were just one of the rest of them," she said with a wink. "Please have a seat, dear." She got up to walk him to a chair. "Let me tell Dr. Diaz you are here. Can I get you anything while you wait?"

"No, thank you, ma'am."

"Okay. You just wait right there, and the principal will be with you in a minute, all right?"

"Yes, ma'am."

She motioned politely to the painter, who stepped aside. As the door opened, Thomas could hear a man having an irate conversation with someone about plumbing in a bathroom. When the door closed, he could still hear muffled yelling.

After a few minutes, the woman came out as the painter finished his artwork on the door. Behind her emerged a portly, balding Hispanic man in his mid-forties wearing the shiniest blue suit Thomas had ever seen. A transplant from a small town in California, the ambitious principal had become enamored with Chicago and its unique way of getting things done. Beads of sweat on his forehead had trickled down his neck, drenching the collar of his starched white shirt.

With a wide grin and a firm handshake, he came right up to Thomas and said, "Mr. Clarke, it is an honor to finally meet you. Please come into my office and make yourself comfortable."

"Thank you, sir."

Principal Diaz took out a handkerchief and wiped his brow, looking over at the door.

"Wayne, great work! Fantastic! Charlene, hold all my calls, please."

The office was voluminous, modern, and smelled of fresh paint. Offering Thomas a large leather chair in front of his desk, the principal went around and opened a manila file containing computer printouts. He nodded approvingly as he skimmed over the pages. "This is very impressive, Mr. Clarke. We are expecting great things from you."

Behind the desk, from floor to ceiling, was a window offering a panoramic view of the meandering Chicago River. Sunlight hit the buildings that emerged from the treetop wilderness, making the different colors of brick more distinctive and vivid by freeing them from the dullness imposed by exposure to weather and time. Simultaneously, all the window reflections from the various buildings burned intensely like fallen stars. The leaves on the trees had not yet begun their autumn turn, so the lush green flora enveloped the river and spread out to cover the entire city until the distant downtown skyscrapers towered into the clouds.

"That is wonderfully beautiful, sir," Thomas remarked.

"Huh?" Dr. Diaz looked around, uncertain what Thomas was referring to.

"Urbs in Horto."

"What?" He finally determined that Thomas was looking out the window. "Oh, yes, I suppose it is nice. I never noticed before. I like that view because it lets me keep an eye on where the real action is," he said while pointing toward the city center. "Anyway, as I said, your record is outstanding, and I am sure you will not disappoint us."

"I will try my best, sir."

"It says here that you won some contests for Latin composition. Lots of students here have enough trouble with English," Dr. Diaz said with a belly laugh before quickly turning serious again. "We don't offer Latin, but we do have a Speech Club and a Debate Club that could use someone of your caliber. Do you have any plans to join them?"

"Yes, I do, sir."

"Good," the principal replied with relief and conviction. "We also offer an AP/Honors Club. It is not easy to get into, but if you are selected to join, you can earn extra credit."

Thomas simply nodded.

"Have you given any thought to what career you would like to get into, Mr. Clarke?"

Thomas smiled and said, "No, sir, I have not thought about that at all."

"You know, with your credentials, you should only be applying to top-tier universities." Dr. Diaz waited for some sort of response but received none. Thomas sat erect, yet he appeared tranquil. "I'll be honest with you, Mr. Clarke. When most students end up sitting in that chair, it usually means they've got themselves into some kind of trouble, and I can be a tough disciplinarian." Still no reaction from this kid. "Because I am only concerned with the future well-being of all my students, I feel the need sometimes to push them. With that in mind, though, I want you to feel like you have a friend in this office. If there is anything I can do for you, just let me know. All right?"

"Yes, sir."

"Mr. Clarke, I want to see you excel here at West Ridge Prep, and I want to help you get into the best university program possible. Now, I have quite a few friends who work in the admissions offices of the universities you need to be in, and if this year goes as well as I expect it to, I am going to have a little talk with them to see what I can do."

"That is very kind of you to offer, sir. It is not necessary, though."

Dr. Diaz's jaw hit the floor. He did not see that coming at all and completely lost his train of thought. "Um . . . uh . . . what?"

"Whatever university I end up attending, sir, I will get into it on my own. However, I sincerely appreciate the offer of help. It was very generous."

Principal Diaz was now completely flustered, and the sweat beads appeared again on his forehead. AP/Honors students usually started frothing at the mouth whenever anyone mentioned anything about getting into a top school. Why was this kid sitting here cool as a cucumber, saying he did not want any help at all? What was going on?

As he fumbled for his soaking wet handkerchief, a small two-way radio on the desk crackled to life. "Engineer Schmitt to Principal Diaz. Over."

"Sir, the first class is going to start soon. With your permission, I would like to go now," Thomas said.

"Uh, yes. Fine. Uh, good luck, Mr. Clarke. Charlene will show you on your way."

"Thank you, sir."

Thomas rose, and the radio blared again. "Engineer Schmitt to Principal Diaz. Over." Then again after a few seconds, "Dr. Diaz, this is Chief Engineer Schmitt. If you are there, please respond. The air-conditioning just went out in the teachers' lounge, and the—"

"All right, Schmitt, I hear you. How long will it take?" Dr. Diaz replied harshly as he watched Thomas exit the room.

There was more muffled yelling as Thomas closed the door behind him and came up to the desk of Chief Administrative Assistant Charlene Wilson. Holding his class list in one hand and his overloaded book bag in the other, he asked if she could point him in the direction of his locker. Of course, she would. She came out from behind her desk, carefully looked over all his classes, and gave him a detailed route for the whole day. She put her hand gently on his back and led him out of the office into the main foyer. A left here and then another left at the end of the hall, and Thomas would have plenty of time before the first bell rang.

He thanked her and waded into the sea of humanity filling the corridor. The sleek and angular interior of the school was pleasant enough to look at, but it also seemed sterile, like a prefabricated office building. It was a maze navigable only by following color-coded directional signs on the walls that matched lines on the floor. In no time, he was at his locker, which opened with a fancy key card. It was easily three times the size of his old locker at St. Titus.

He tossed his things inside and checked his watch. Ten minutes until class. Simultaneously fighting the crowd and following the lines would take most of that time. He pivoted, looking for an opening in the perpetual flow of traffic. An indistinct wall rushed past, gaudy, loud, and entirely oblivious to him. One last check of his morning classes: history in 1403, calculus in 604, then homeroom in 842.

"Thomas?"

The voice cut through the noise and mayhem, and he turned immediately, searching for its source. He would know that voice anywhere.

"Thomas?"

Marie Martin came toward him, the radiant smile on her face growing with each approaching step.

"Thomas!"

She placed her book bag on the floor, wrapped her arms around him, and almost squeezed the life out of him. "Thomas, I can't believe you are really here," she said into his ear.

"Marie!" was all he could get out because he could not breathe.

The last time they had seen each other, on graduation day three years prior, she had given him a hug like that, but they were children then. Somehow she managed to give him one last squeeze even harder than the first before releasing him and looking him over from head to toe.

"Look at how tall you are!" she exclaimed, amazed that he had at least three inches on her five-foot-eight-inch frame.

As a young child, Marie had been long and thin in a gangly way. Her maternal grandmother, Josephine Bertrand, a very elegant and refined woman, had insisted that her children and grandchildren learn proper manners. As Marie grew physically, she increased also in gracefulness, studying ballet and piano. Grandmother Bertrand always claimed they were descendants of ancient French nobility, not so much as in possessing a title but rather as in possessing a quality. If true, Marie would make a fine example of a young lady of *l'Ancien Régime*—modest in manner with fair and delicate features. Thomas had to catch himself from gazing too long at her flowing dark brown hair and her stunning green eyes.

Pulchritudinous was the only word his Latin-soaked mind could come up with, so he thought it best to say nothing.

"Thomas, I am so happy you are here. How is your family?"

"They are all well. Thank you for asking. How is your mom?" Thomas replied politely, venturing into delicate territory.

"Fine, thanks. Let me see your class list." Marie was bursting with joy. "We have the same morning classes and homeroom. Come on," she said as she took his hand, "the bell is going to ring. I will show you the way."

Thomas closed his locker and followed, not that he had a choice in the matter. Marie did not ease up on his hand until they had entered room 1403. He paused to catch his breath and noticed everyone staring at Marie and the smile she could not contain. She kept talking only with Thomas and did not pay any attention to the other students in the room.

CHAPTER 3

After the second-period calculus class let out, Thomas and Marie made their way into the hallway. She gently took his arm, in a way more accustomed to her nature, and pulled him close so that they could talk in confidence.

"So, what do you think?"

"It's okay."

She gave him a frown. When Marie Martin was five years old, she began taking piano lessons from Thomas's mother in the Clarke family's living room. From the first moment they had met, Thomas and Marie shared a special bond, souls of a like nature drawn toward each other. While Thomas had many other friends, only God Almighty understood him better than Marie, and Marie felt the same way about Thomas. Thomas had always been reserved in public about what he said and who he said it to, so she tugged softly on his arm and asked again, "What do you think?"

Her prodding made him laugh, and he answered quietly, "I was concerned at first because this school is very selective. I will do my best, though, to persevere in the face of adversity." She smiled as they slowly moved further on. Thomas asked, "Was it my imagination, or was there one guy sitting in the front row of both classes who was giving me the evil eye?"

"No, that was not you imagination. That was Scott Weber. He is very . . . ambitious."

"Oh boy. Petrarch would say that envy persecutes those who are ambitious. The less you strive for glory, the more you will obtain it."

"Yes, that is true, but Scott is also the president of the AP/Honors Club, which I would like you to join, please."

"Dr. Diaz mentioned something about applying for that. If all the members in this club are like Scott Weber, I am sure it will be great."

"Oh, stop! Most of the people in it are from our last two classes. Only juniors and seniors can apply. It's really just an extra hour of study time after school, although on Fridays you can make some kind of short presentation for extra credit. You'll like it."

"Well, if it's only one hour."

She squeezed his arm, and they walked toward their homeroom as if no time had passed between them at all. Thomas looked around at the different groups surging through the hallways. Most appeared harmless; others were more foul and vulgar, with their profanities ignored by the faculty and security guards. Marie Martin did not belong in this place.

"How have you gotten along here, Marie?"

"Um. . . . "

A voice boomed from behind them, "Well, well, well. The Lone Ranger and Tonto ride again." Thomas turned, recognizing the sharply toned utterances of Richard J. McGee, who continued on, "She's been like peanut butter without jelly, moping around here for the past three years with sad puppy dog eyes because her hero, Tommy Clarke, was at St. Titus winning football championships."

"Oh, Richard," Marie said to chastise him.

"Richie McGee, how are you?" Thomas shook his hand, glad to see another friend from grammar school.

Tall and lanky, Richard McGee had always possessed an outgoing personality. It was not until the fifth grade, though, that he began to apply himself as a topflight smart aleck. While the nuns at St. Titus had kept him on a short leash, outside of school, his razor-sharp mind became finely attuned to the nuanced art of making people feel uncomfortable.

When he came to West Ridge for high school, the discipline of the Catholic schools was gone completely. He terrorized both the student body and the faculty, and there was nothing anyone could do about it. Being in AP/Honors, he could handle any of the academic requirements. More importantly, though, he was the son of State Representative Charles McGee, chairman of the House Education Committee. This committee was responsible for the building and continued funding of West Ridge Prep. Richard McGee was untouchable, and most everyone, from the principal down to the lowliest freshman, was simply counting the days until he left.

"So, has Marie shown you the ropes, or has she just made goo-goo eyes all morning long?"

"Richard," Marie began, not letting him try her patience.

Thomas quickly interjected, "I've only been here for two classes, so why don't you fill me in, please?"

"Well, for the most part, you have the flotsam and jetsam that make up the majority of our great nation." Sarcasm was imbued in Richard McGee's bones. "Yes sir, all races, cultures, and creeds combining into the ever discordant and wavering multitude, the beast with many heads, the *profanus vulgus*, if you will." He was building toward a full-blown rant. "These are the idiots who believe what they read on the Internet and think that characters on television shows and in the movies are real. These morons—"

"Hold on, Rich. You are going to hyperventilate," Thomas said.

"Sorry." Richard took a deep breath and got back on topic. "About two-thirds of the students here are in Honors classes; the rest are in AP/Honors. Keep in mind, though, if these regular Honors students were at St. Ti's, they would be in the special needs class with the mentally challenged kids. But they get the same diploma that we do." Before Thomas could say anything in reproach, Richard held up his hand to acknowledge that he realized he had gone too far.

"All they care about here are test scores, and that is where the AP/Honors students come in. If we keep our 4.0 GPAs and do well on the state tests for reading and mathematics, everyone is happy."

Richard had a tendency to exaggerate, and usually it was easy to tell when he did, but it was not entirely clear to Thomas this time. Thomas looked at Marie, who was unusually quiet.

"You don't believe me, do you?" Richard asked.

"Rich, as I have said, I have only been here for two classes."

"Well, I am sure by now that you have met Principal Diaz and that he has promised you the world. He did that because he knows what your grades and test scores will mean to the school's averages and state rankings. A change of even a fraction of a percentage point in those averages could move us from number five to number one or to number ten in the rankings. That means a lot to a guy with inflated political aspirations. He could not care less if you or anyone else here learned anything about your beloved virtue."

Thomas still looked doubtful, and Richard continued.

"What did they teach us at St. Titus about the difference between vocation and career? Vocation is based on using whatever gifts and talents you have to serve and love God and to serve and love neighbor. Whether you are a garbage collector or a ditch digger or the president of the United States, it does not matter. Everyone has different gifts, and they should use them to their fullest to serve the public good, right? Meanwhile, career is based on self and using your talents to serve yourself and advance yourself. This place is all about career. Everyone here is looking out for themselves. One mention of virtue, ethics, or morals would bring an ACLU goon squad in here with lawsuits and injunctions. The school doesn't want any part of that."

Marie did speak up to say that the AP/Honors teachers were generally very good and that the curriculum in the AP program was challenging. Richard conceded those two points.

"All I am trying to say is, Tom, you are in a whole different place now, and you shook up everything here when you transferred in."

"Really?"

"Of course, because you aced the ACT, and everyone here knows it."

"How do they know that?" Thomas asked with concern.

"Well, Marie and I knew it from the St. Titus old woman gossip vine. Everyone else found out when they hacked into your computer file." Richard held up his hand again to prevent Thomas from protesting, then continued. "You are the first person to transfer into AP/Honors as a senior, and there is a pecking order around here based on the grades and test scores. They were desperate to know where you were going to fit in. Everyone here scored in the low thirties on the ACT. You were one of only 592 people in the whole country to get a 36. That sent them all into a tizzy, and you knocked Mr. Fantastic Scotty Weber—and his 34—out of the top spot. Now he is scared to death that you are going to be valedictorian."

"I am here to learn, not to be valedictorian."

"That is my point exactly. Scotty Fabulous would cut off his own toes to be valedictorian. It is incomprehensible to him to think otherwise. You get good grades because you want to learn and because you desire to amass all different kinds of knowledge and incorporate that knowledge into a life of virtue. St. Titus wanted us to be well-rounded individuals who could think logically, reasonably, ethically, and morally. Here at West Ridge Prep, it's only numbers and rankings. The people here have some good qualities too, but never having studied philosophy or theology, they were not taught to think like you do. This is a different world, and now you are in their world."

Although Richard's reasoning was impressive, Thomas was still uncertain if he should believe what had been said. This was the same old Richard McGee, but something was different. He was more bitter.

"So you were paying attention in grammar school," Thomas asked, trying to lighten things up, "when you weren't shooting spitballs at Sr. de Paul?"

That got a grin out of Richard, who replied, "Yes, surprisingly some of it did sink in, and no, I will never admit to the infamous sixth-grade spitball incident."

As the three came up to the homeroom, Richard asked Thomas with surprising honesty, "So, what did I miss at St. Titus over the past three years?"

"Well, apart from Latin, Greek, theology, and philosophy, our regular curriculum at St. Titus was the same as the AP curriculum here. So the difference freshman year would have been Old Testament, New Testament, Homer, and Sophocles. Sophomore year was the Church Fathers and *The Aeneid*. Last year was Plato, St. Augustine, and the first year of Greek. We read all the classical Roman authors, and quite a few medieval ones, in Latin. This year I missed out on Aristotle, St. Thomas Aquinas, and a second year of Greek. I have a feeling I may regret suggesting it, but if you are looking for something to read, I think you would most enjoy Plato and the Socratic method of dialectic."

"Thanks," Richard said. Something in the hallway caught Richard's eye. He gave Marie a look and asked

Thomas in a more jovial manner, "So, Tom Bomb, are you going to play football this year?"

"I am going to try out."

"Well, just so you know, last year they stunk, and the main reason why they stunk is standing right over there." Richard nodded across the hall to a short, flabby young man dressed in cargo pants, sandals, and a wrinkled T-shirt. His hair hung down into his eyes, and he flipped it back and forth as he shifted his weight from one leg to another.

"That is Rex Burger. The hyper little gnat next to him is his sidekick, Steve Souter."

"I am sure you all are the best of friends," Thomas quipped.

"Souter is harmless. He just follows around Maximus Rex Puga. Did I get that right?" Richard was uncertain of his Latin.

"I get the general idea."

"Burger is a typical northwest side meathead; he's fat and ignorant, yet he has a very high opinion of his opinion. He also cries like a little girl. Oh, watch this! Here comes Donald Spears."

"Hey, Rexsh. Hey, Schteve. How are you, my friendsch?" Spears asked, showcasing what he believed to be his cool way of speaking.

"Yeah, I'm cool, Spears," Rex said as he shifted to the other leg and flipped his hair.

"You know, I schtill can't get over the scheaschon you had lascht year. It wasch incredible."

"Rex kicked ass last year," Steve chimed in with enthusiasm.

"I was outstanding last year. Actually, I am surprised I haven't done anything that incredible in a while. This year's season is going to start soon, though, and I've been working out with a personal trainer all summer. I'm probably in the best shape of my life right now."

"Rexsh, that is schimply fantaschtic, my friend."

"Yeah, Rex is going to kick even more ass this year," Steve chimed in again.

With a disgusted look on his face, Richard told Thomas, "My stomach can't take any more of this. I am going to show you why their record was 0 and 8 last year."

He slowly circled back and came up behind Rex Burger. When the first homeroom bell rang, Rex shifted to his left leg. Richard barely touched the back of Rex's knee, and the fulcrum holding up all of Rex's weight collapsed. As his books flew up in the air and his torso came crashing down, Rex let out a horrified, high-pitched screech. Heads turned throughout the hallway to look for the source of the effeminate wailing.

"Oh, Rex! I did not see you! I am terribly sorry!" Richard exclaimed with feigned concern.

"What are you trying to do, McGee? Break my leg? Steve, go get the nurse." His voice was still very high pitched and sniveling. Steve stood in shock until Rex shouted again, "Steve, move!" Steve hesitated and looked around frantically before he finally took off running.

"Rex, it is entirely my fault. I was not looking, and I bumped into you by accident. I am really sorry."

"You'd better be sorry, McGee." Rex noticed a crowd gathering around, laughing, so he held his knee and rocked back and forth. "I think I heard my ACL snap."

"Wow, it's a good thing you are in such great shape, Rex. Your rehab should only be about seven or eight months. Come on, let me help you up."

"Don't touch me, McGee. My leg needs a traction splint."

Richard rolled his eyes and said under his breath, "What a pansy! I have got to get to homeroom."

Steve came up with the nurse and a wheelchair. Richard turned his back on the dramatics, shaking his head and saying, "I can't believe he's the most popular kid in school."

Richard came up to Thomas and Marie, feeling proud of himself and full of vigor. He declared, "Yes, sir, this is a different world, Tommy Boy. At least Princess Marie has her little sweetie pie with her again." Richard started to make kissing noises until Thomas came up uncomfortably close with a serious look in his eye.

"Rich, we have been friends for a long time, and we have always kidded each other. I don't have any problem with that. Marie is not one of the guys, and she is not your enemy. You can make fun of me all you want, but you leave her alone." Thomas did not raise his voice, but he was unmistakably firm.

"You're right, you're right, you're right. Marie, I am sorry." Richard knew he was acting like a child and had once again gotten carried away. "I apologize to you both." He was sincere, but he was also still full of energy, so he turned around and kicked open the door to the homeroom. The pneumatic closer broke into pieces, and the door flew open, slamming into the wall with a loud crash. Everyone in the room snapped to attention as Richard McGee announced with a commanding voice, "Listen up, pinheads! There's a new sheriff in town."

Marie had been embarrassed by Richard. Thomas stopped her before she entered the room and said, "You know how he can be. Don't let him get to you. I missed you, Marie, and I am very happy to see you again."

Now she was embarrassed for a completely different reason, but her beaming smile returned. Thomas was here, and everything was going to be all right.

CHAPTER 4

Margaret Clarke loved gardening, and to no one's surprise, she was having another bumper crop of vegetables. When she wasn't running the household, volunteering at church, giving piano lessons, or helping her husband at his work, she was in her garden. As a child, her mother had impressed upon her how fortunate it was to be able to grow your own food and provide for yourself in good times and bad. That turned out to be very practical advice when the price of food skyrocketed earlier that year, and this simple garden helped her save a tremendous amount of money. Over half of the Clarke backyard was brimming with carrots, green beans, spinach, peas, and tomatoes.

Carefully looking over each well-ordered row, she had to decide which should be taken for dinner and which should be taken for canning. The sounds of Kathleen's piano practice drill wafted through the window as Margaret selected four tomatoes to save for the winter.

Coming into the kitchen, she checked the chicken in the oven, the boiling rice, and the steaming carrots, then began to follow the canning instructions for tomatoes in an old *Better Homes and Gardens* cookbook. She looked out the window, trying to think of some place to put an apple tree. A groan from her husband in the dining room made her put everything aside for the moment.

Coming up behind him, she put a hand on his shoulder and could feel the tension in his neck. John had told her earlier about the annual property taxes on the business jumping from $24,000 to $32,000. Now he had just found out that the property taxes on their home were going up by $1,800 as well. This came right after signing a $400 check to the gas company as part of the payment plan for last winter's heating bill. Autumn was right around the corner, and this year's winter would soon follow.

"Hans came over today and told me that Jack Philbin sold his building to a developer and was moving out to the suburbs," John said with a hint of melancholy in his voice. "Hans also told me that someone from the alderman's office came into his shop and told him flat out that the alderman wanted his building and was going to get it. Jack had owned the building to the north of us for twenty-five years, and Hans had been to the south since the sixties. Hans has no intention of selling, but he is worried about the city using eminent domain to take his property." Margaret caressed her husband's neck and kissed him on the cheek as Thomas came down from his room.

"Dad, did you hear that a group of medal winners from the Beijing Olympics are going to at Brooks Park this weekend? Michael Phelps is going to be there."

John was distracted, but Kathleen immediately stopped her playing and said enthusiastically, "I have step dancing at Brooks this weekend. Maybe we will see some of them."

"We can try to find out what time they will be there, dear," Margaret replied as her husband nodded in agreement. John was lost in his thoughts, but the soft touch of his wife's hand through his hair brought him back to the matters at present. He looked over at the crucifix hanging on the dining room wall and then back at his wife. Kathleen and Thomas both had a good first day of school, and the family would soon share a delicious meal together.

"You certainly don't get to meet Olympic gold medal winners every day," John said as he cleaned up the bills and pulled the Liturgy of the Hours out of a drawer. "Okay, we have enough time for the Evening Prayer before dinner. Tom, will you start, please?"

***

"When the final bell of the final class finally rings, freedom is finally felt," Geoffrey Spencer said as he checked the clock on the wall. "Anyone?"

That had not been part of any assigned reading, and all he saw before him were blank stares, venturing toward panic. Good. These kids were so intelligent and wrapped up so tight that every once in a while they needed something to shake them up.

"It's a wonderful example of alliteration, and it is also a true statement. Can anyone tell me the source of that quote and how it ties in with what we have been discussing?"

A few brave souls meekly threw out vague comparisons to Keats and Kipling. The tension in the room was thick, so Mr. Spencer let them off the hook.

"The quote was from Geoffrey Spencer, West Ridge Prep, senior English class, fall 2008. It was off the top of my head, and I admit it was not exactly a wonderful example of alliteration, but it was all I could come up with on short notice." The class let out a collective sigh of relief. "The point I have been trying to make is this: challenge yourself to think about literature in new ways. Thank you for the Keats comparison, though."

Thomas was impressed. Although he missed Latin and some of his other classes, the first two weeks at West Ridge had been challenging, and he was certain his intellect would get a workout over the next eight months. The only other trick would be to find time for work at his dad's shop, football, the debate and speech teams, and spending time with his family and Marie while still having some time for himself.

"Next week we begin *Beowulf,* using Heaney, so you can see the old Anglo-Saxon text next to a modern translation. I want to have the introduction and the first fifty pages done by next Friday. Have a good weekend, everyone."

As the students collected their belongings and filed out of the room, Mr. Spencer saw a note on his desk. "Mr. Clarke, could you come here, please?"

Thomas walked up to the front of the room, and a piece of paper dropped to the floor. Mr. Spencer bent down to retrieve it. As he tried to get up, his face flushed and then turned pale. He staggered before catching himself.

"Are you all right, sir?"

"Yes, yes, I'm fine. Thank you. Just a little lightheaded. I am not as young as I think I am. Dr. Diaz would like to see you, Mr. Clarke." He handed Thomas the slip of paper, still looking glassy eyed.

"Thank you, sir. Are you sure everything is okay?"

"Never better. You know, Mr. Clark, I have been meaning to ask you something. Are you related in any way to John Clarke, the printer from St. Titus?"

"Yes, sir. That is my father."

"I thought there was a resemblance. I grew up in St. Bridget, but I was a year behind your father in high school at St. Titus. He was a fine man. I hope he is doing well. Sorry to hear about the school."

"Thank you, sir. He is doing well. I will tell him you asked for him."

"Please do, Mr. Clarke." Even though he was struggling to catch his breath, Mr. Spencer rejected the offers of help and told Thomas to get to the principal's office.

Richard was waiting at the door. "I thought the old guy was going to blow a gasket. What's this all about?" Richard pointed to the note in Thomas's hand.

"Dr. Diaz wants to see me again."

"This is, what, the fifth time in two weeks? There is something going on with that guy. I am going to find out what diabolical scheme he is cooking up for you, Batman. Later."

"Thanks."

When Thomas walked into the principal's office, the secretary jumped up. "Hello, Thomas. It's so nice to see you again. Please have a seat. Can I get you anything?"

"No, thank you, ma'am."

"You just wait right there. Dr. Diaz is on a very important phone call right now." She looked around as if someone might be hiding in her little cubicle and whispered, "It's the mayor." She put her finger to her lips and made a buttoning motion, urging Thomas not to reveal the vital national security secret she had just disclosed. "He'll be with you in a minute." She winked at him and returned to her desk.

Thomas let out a sigh and checked his watch. Five minutes to three. From his seat against the wall, he could hear Dr. Diaz saying he was fully committed to the mayor's education platform. "You have my word; I will deliver. West Ridge is the most racially diverse, highest scoring school in the state. There is nothing to worry about." After a groveling salutation, the phone slammed down.

A minute later, the door opened and Thomas was called in. Dr. Diaz took in a deep breath and quickly let it out. "Please sit down, Mr. Clarke. How are you?"

"Fine. Thank you, sir."

"I have been getting fantastic reports on your work so far. Outstanding. Keep it up. The reason, though, that I called you here today was that I heard you are going to try out for football. Is that correct?"

"Yes, sir. It is."

"Well, we have never had an AP/Honors student play a varsity sport before, and I am a little concerned."

"Sir, I played football for three years at my old school and was able to keep my grades up. It will not be any different here."

The principal gave him a long look. "Well, all right. I don't want anything to interfere with your schoolwork, though."

"I understand. Thank you, sir. I have a presentation to make right now to get into the AP/Honors Club. So, unless there is anything else, may I be excused?"

"Wonderful. Let me write you a note. Normally, I attend many of those, but I have some pressing business here. Good luck."

"Thank you, sir."

Ricardo Diaz watched Thomas take the note and exit the room. Why did this kid make him so nervous? He could not put his finger on it. After waiting to hear the outer door close, he hit the intercom and commanded, "Charlene, make sure I am receiving biweekly status reports on Thomas Clarke."

"Yes, Dr. Diaz."

Before the principal could sit down, a call came in on the radio about a leak in the glass dome of the atrium.

***

"Honey, don't worry about me. I am fine, and the business will get through this," John said, trying to ease his wife's growing concern. St. Aloysius University, one of his biggest customers, was cutting back on their advertising budget by 40 percent. "We have gone through rough stretches in the past, and we will get through this one. The university has been a longtime customer, and when things pick up again, so will their orders. They are decent people over there." He heard a commotion in front of the shop but could not see anything out the window.

"Margaret, I have to go. I will call you later. I love you."

CHAPTER 4

As John came to the front door, he saw an overweight, middle-aged black woman in a poorly fitting blue-and-white polyester Chicago Fire Department uniform. She was getting out of a brand-new, candy apple red Mercedes Benz convertible. Her head was too big for her body and her white officer's hat. She was screaming into a cell phone. "Listen, girl, ain't no way they're going to take away my mileage check. I want my money. I don't care what's right or what's wrong. I don't care what the law says. I am going to do whatever I have to do to cover my ass. That's what we do as inspectors."

She flipped the phone shut and came up to the front door of Clarke Printing. "Good morning. How are you doing today, sir? My name is Lieutenant Hosanna Travers, and I am here to do a fire inspection of this premise. You cannot deny me entry, and you must accompany me for the duration of the inspection, okay?" She hiked up her pants halfway up her torso and entered.

"Please come in."

She looked over a sheet of paper on a clipboard. "Now, this is Clarke Printing and you are Patrick Clarke?" She pronounced his name "Clark-ee."

"This is Clarke Printing, but my name is John Clarke. My father has not owned the business for many years."

"I see. Now, you should have informed the inspectors who came here in the past to update that information." John Clarke had, in fact, told every single inspector who had been there for over two decades. She looked over her sheet and continued, "Are the address and phone number correct?"

"Yes, they are."

"All right, sir." She began to wander aimlessly through the building.

"Ma'am, if I may, we have one exit in front and one directly out the back. Both are kept unlocked during business hours. We have one extinguisher up by the office, one in the middle here, and one by the back door. The tags are all up to date. Our heating and air-conditioning are on the roof."

"Sir, I am the fire inspector, and I will conduct this investigation the way I see fit. Please do not tell me how to do my job. You are being disruptive. I feel at this time I must inform you of that information, okay? Now, what is it you do here, sir?"

"This is a print shop."

"Where is your sprinkler system and fire pump?"

"We don't have one, ma'am.

She looked confused. "Okay, what are you saying now?"

"To my knowledge, there has never been a sprinkler system in this building."

She was still confused. "Sir, according to my paperwork, there is a sprinkler system and a fire pump on this premise, and they will need to be checked because they are very important in regards to the egress from this premise."

"Ma'am, look. You can see the wooden truss for the roof right above us. If there was a sprinkler system here, there would be pipes and sprinkler heads visible. There are none."

With a pained look on her face, she checked something off with a red pen on the paper she was holding.

"Uh-huh. Okay. Now, what is this here?"

"That is a floor drain."

"Why does it look like that? When was the last time you had it checked out?"

"I don't understand. Checked out for what? That has been here since the building was put up eighty years ago. No one has ever checked it for anything because it works fine."

"I don't like the way it looks. You are going to have to get that checked out."

John looked at George, who had no idea what she was talking about.

"Now, what is this here?"

"That is acetone, which we use to clean some of the machines. We have one quart of that. Everything else we have is nonflammable."

"Uh-huh. All right, sir. Well, thank you for your time. Job well done."

After she left, George came up to his boss and said, "The arrogance of ignorance. That's got nothing but trouble written all over it."

CHAPTER 5

Thomas was ten minutes late to make his application speech for the AP/Honors Club. Hurrying from the principal's office, he saw Marie standing in the hallway. She was mildly upset. Marie Martin had experienced considerable disappointment in her life recently, and Thomas knew this was important to her.

"I had to see Dr. Diaz. I have a note. I have worked on this speech for a week, Marie. I will not let you down."

Thomas entered and stood behind a podium at the front of the classroom. His peers sat stone-faced as he began.

"What man prefers misery and wretchedness over happiness? What man seeks distress in his soul over peace? What man choses slavery for himself over freedom? None. None with any sense. The question then becomes, how does one attain happiness, peace, and freedom? Many would have you believe that vice and wickedness are the proper paths to follow. Only an ignorant fool believes this. Others will say, try to be good, but if you fall into some evil, don't worry about it. Cicero would counter that one cannot ask for moderation in vice. One microscopic germ is all that is needed to enter a body and deform it or destroy it. Vice affects the soul in the same manner. So how does one achieve happiness, peace, and freedom? The only reasonable answer is the perfection of virtue. In the short time we have today, I will present a brief description of the four cardinal virtues: prudence, justice, temperance, and fortitude.

"Prudence is the application of wisdom in judgment. A wise man chooses what is good, just, and true. How does he do that? By knowing, loving, and imitating God who is the Supreme Good. These are the words of St. Augustine, but let me also cite the words of Plato, a pagan Greek. According to Plato, 'There are two patterns set up in reality. One is the divine and supremely happy. The other has nothing of God in it and is the deepest unhappiness.'

"Justice is giving the good God and our fellow man their proper due, in that order. Temperance, or moderation, will not allow passions or emotions to cloud proper judgment. Fortitude is moral courage to do what is good, just, and true.

"Plato gives us a further understanding of the relationship between justice and temperance. That which is of a higher nature must command that which is of a lower nature; this is the natural order. In every way possible, God is of the highest nature. For there to be peace and order in all of creation, God must command all things. Acknowledging this natural order and giving God his proper due is the exercise of justice.

"But we can also see the importance of the natural order on a lower level. For example, who wishes to live in a neighborhood, a city, or a country where there is no order? If a gang of thugs attempted to overthrow the authority of a legitimate government and disregard legitimate laws, disorderly conduct and disturbances of the peace would follow, such as riots or insurrections. We see this activity every day in our own neighborhoods. For there to be peace, the natural order of things must be in place. Laws must be obeyed, and legitimate government must command because they are, by nature, of a natural higher authority than drug dealers and criminals. By the same token, a government—or any organization for that matter—can only be successful if it has the best and most capable people in positions of leadership, no matter if it is a mayor, a king, the captain of a ship, or the CEO of a company. Those who are most able to lead must lead; otherwise order will break down, and chaos will ensue. Order is preferable to disorder in every instance.

"It follows that each individual soul must also be properly ordered as well. Similar natures tend toward one another. That which is of a higher nature tends toward others that are of a higher nature, and that of a lower nature tends toward others of a lower nature. Reason and love reside in the immortal soul and seek changeless, perfect, eternal truth. Passions, emotions, and sensual desires are of the mortal body and seek the lowly, base, and finite. The soul strives for the divine; the body strives for the earthly.

"If a soul is commanded by desires for food, drink, sex, money, status, power, material possessions, or any vice, then the natural command of reason and love is upended, and the soul is thrown into disorder and chaos like a rudderless ship being tossed in a storm. The soul is quickly overcome by these vices and becomes enslaved to them, and they are cruel masters. A soul in this condition willingly commits the most disgraceful and dishonorable acts to serve its masters because this soul has convinced itself that it is not enslaved. Those oppressed by a tyrant or held in physical bondage by another human being are in positions imposed on them by another. There can be no doubt that these individuals are enslaved. Self-deception and self-delusion, however, are as easy as breathing. Because this slavery to the passions is self-imposed, it is the vilest kind of slavery.

"Balance is best in all things. Only the well-ordered soul brings peace, happiness, and freedom. Reason and love must command the passions, emotions, and bodily desires, for a rational, loving soul is what sets us apart from the brute animals. This is the exercise of temperance and justice.

"Virgil writes that if the passions are not controlled by reason, they would sweep away the earth, sea, and sky. St. Paul teaches that the soul is weighed down by a body destined to die. Horace would advise us then, as young men and women, that now is our time for learning and coming to understand the obligations of adulthood. So let us orient ourselves toward truth.

"Virtue is the art of proper living. Virtue brings balance and order. A properly ordered soul brings happiness, peace, and freedom. What man seeks foolishness over wisdom? Who strives for injustice over justice? Rashness and intemperance over moderation? Fear over courage? Falsehood over truth? Only the ignorant believe what is false, but one must be both ignorant and prideful to assert lies and falsehoods impudently. Pride is based on the lie that mortal man is of a higher nature than God, while humility is nothing more than the acceptance of unchanging, eternal truth. When one possesses the perfect, why would one exchange it for the imperfect? Let us leave behind, then, the imperfect that brings discord, sadness, and enslavement and strive only for that which is perfect and gives an overabundance of happiness, peace, and freedom.

"Petrarch, describing the woman he loved and could never have for his own, tells of she who desires heavenly, eternal things, in whose appearance there shines the pattern of divine beauty, whose ways form a perfect model of honor. Her voice and glance have nothing mortal in them." Thomas quickly looked over at Marie, then continued.

"There is much more that could be said, but I will leave you with the words of a wise and holy man: 'Whatever is true, whatever is honorable, whatever is pure, whatever is lovely, whatever is gracious, if there is any excellence, if there is anything worthy of praise, think about these things.' Thank you."

Thomas collected his papers. The room was full of wide eyes and silence. Marie came up, elated. "That was very well said, Thomas, and wonderful." She had heard him make speeches like this before, but she had never been more proud of him than she was today.

"Thank you, Marie," Thomas replied before checking his watch. As the classroom quietly emptied for a break before the deliberations began on Thomas's acceptance, a short and very young looking boy came up with a taller girl behind him. Marie introduced William Donohue, a senior, and his sister, Susan, a junior.

"It is a pleasure to meet you," William said as he extended his hand formally and awkwardly. Thomas shook his hand while Susan gave a quiet, polite "hello." William stood in silence for a moment, quickly looking back and forth between Thomas and Marie.

"Thomas, I must say, when Marie approached the club about the possibility of your admittance, I was among those who thought the idea untenable. A senior transfer student into the AP/Honors Club is without precedent."

Thomas held in a smile and nodded his head.

"But after hearing your speech," William continued, "Marie's delineations of your cognitive abilities were not incredulous. I should not have doubted; Marie has never been a fabulist. I would like you to know that I am going to vigorously pursue your acceptance into this club." With a look of great determination, he firmly shook Thomas's hand again. "In the future, I would like to discuss further some of the things you spoke of today."

"Thank you, William. I appreciate that very much, and I look forward to talking with you. Will you all please excuse me? Football starts next week, and I have to take a physical this afternoon. Marie, will you please call me later and let me know how the club voted?"

Marie nodded and asked, "What time will you be home?"

"This should not take too long. It's 3:30 now. I should be home by five at the latest."

"I shall talk to you then."

After saying their good-byes, Marie, William, and Susan eagerly returned to the club to decide if Thomas would be let in, and Thomas headed toward the nurse's office for his physical.

CHAPTER 6

He came up to the nurse's office exactly on time. There was no nurse, but he did recognize the only other student in the room.

"Hi. I am Thomas Clarke."

"Steve Souter." He was a bundle of nerves, slight of build, and four inches shorter than Thomas. Steve's brown hair was closely cropped, spiked in front with blond highlights. He did not look like a conversationalist, but this might be a future teammate, so Thomas made an effort.

"Do you have a 3:30 appointment also?

"Yeah."

"Do you know what the holdup is?"

"No."

"Have you seen the nurse?"

"Nope."

Steve looked nervously around the room. *What could make him so jumpy?* Thomas wondered.

Thomas and Steve watched the nurse walk very slowly into the room, sit down, and begin to shuffle through some papers in front of her. After a few minutes of complete silence, she stood up.

"Rex Burger, Thomas Clarke, and Steven Souter?"

"I'm Thomas Clarke."

"I'm Steven Souter. Rex is not here yet. He's on his way."

"Well, we will wait for him then."

"Excuse me, ma'am, is there any way Steven or I could start now while we are waiting?"

"No." The nurse looked over the papers on her desk a few more times, then got up and very slowly walked out of the room.

More silence. Thomas checked his watch. It was closing in on four o'clock. He had promised his dad that he would work a few hours tonight, and he wanted to have some time to eat dinner before going to the shop. His did not want to miss the call from Marie, either. As much as his joining the AP/Honors Club meant to her, the extra hour of quiet study time before football practice would be a big help. More time with Marie would also be welcome.

The wait was trying, but there was nothing he could do about it, so Thomas pulled out his copy of *The Confessions of St. Augustine* and began to read. Steve glanced over at Thomas and then searched around for something to read, finally becoming engrossed in a pamphlet on eczema. When Rex Burger finally showed up at ten minutes after four, Steve jumped out of his seat.

"Hey, Rex. What's up, dude? What took so long? The nurse was getting pissed."

"Take it easy. I have been code brown for the last twenty-five minutes. Man, I don't know what it is, but sometimes when I drink a Coke in the afternoon, it makes me have to cop a squat like you cannot believe." Rex was an inch taller than Steve but forty pounds heavier. Sauntering in the room with a hair flip, he went on for the next few moments to give graphic details of his latest adventure in the bathroom.

"Yeah, me too, Rex. Sometimes even carbonated water does it to me."

"Man, why do you drink that sissy water?"

"I don't know. My mom always buys it. She thinks it's healthy or something."

"I drink a liter of Coke every day, and I am in great shape. I don't believe all that 'water is healthier' stuff."

"Yeah, I love Coke, especially with greasy food like a gyro or a cheeseburger."

"Man, I am starving right now, Steve. When we get out of here, I am going to need a meatball grinder pronto."

"Man, that sounds great."

"Then we'll get a case of Coors and head back to my basement. I got some stuff there, too."

"Yeah, Rex! I want to get freaking wasted tonight, dude."

"Hell yeah. What is taking this broad so long?"

The nurse appeared and made her slow return to the desk. After a few more minutes of looking over the papers again, she called out, "Rex Burger, Thomas Clarke, and Steven Souter?"

Thomas jumped up and said, "Yes, ma'am."

"You are all required to go to the Axis Testing Facility to receive your physical. Do any of you have access to a vehicle?"

"Yeah, I got my new Tahoe," Rex said with a hair flip.

"Then you are required to drive the others to the facility and return. Here is the address. It closes in one hour."

Thomas thought about going on his own, but the facility was a few miles away, and a ride would be faster.

"Hi. I'm Thomas Clarke. I hope you don't mind—"

"Whatever. Let's just go."

Thomas followed Rex and Steve out to the parking lot and a shiny, jet black Chevy Tahoe. Rex and Steve went to the front seats, and it took a few seconds for Rex to unlock the back door. Thomas climbed up into the cavernous rear seat that still smelled new.

"This is quite a car," Thomas marveled, noticing all the added extras.

"First of all, it's an SUV. Second, it better be nice because it cost forty-eight grand." Rex turned the ignition, and the huge, 320 horsepower V8 engine roared to life.

"Rex, you are going to score so bad with this ride. Can we hook up your iPod and crank some tunes?" Steve asked, rubbing the leather trim.

"No, there is something wrong with the stereo. The stupid dealer has to fix it." (In actuality, Rex had blown out the speakers a few days earlier.)

Rex shifted into neutral, gunning the engine, then dropped the gear shift into drive. All three passengers were pinned to their seats as the behemoth lurched forward. Thomas kept a firm grip on the door handle and noticed he was the only one wearing a seat belt. It should only be fifteen minutes to the test facility, and he could walk home from there if he had to. Tearing out of the parking lot and into the street, Rex hit the corners fast and hard, swaying the vehicle back and forth. Steve loved it.

"Rex, this is just like the Tahoe they had on *The Real World.*"

"Yeah, but this one is a little better. I have the sunroof and the heated backseats."

"This is going to be just like it was on *The Real World*, driving around Hollywood and getting wasted all the time. This is going to totally rock."

"Damn straight, dude," Rex agreed as he looked around the front seat frantically.

"You know, we should try out for the cast of the next *Real World*, Rex."

Rex was still distracted, searching for something, and paid no attention to the road. "Well, I should probably try out because I have the car already. Man, where is my sports drink?"

Thomas carefully watched the events unfold.

"Yeah, you would get on that show for sure, getting wasted with all those chicks."

"Man, I would love to. There it is."

As Rex reached for the bottle under his seat, Thomas yelled, "Look out!"

Out of the corner of his eye, Rex saw a blur in front of him and hit the brakes hard. The front seat passengers screamed and flew forward as six thousand pounds of steel screeched to a halt a few inches from a pickup truck piled fifteen feet high with junk. A stove, a refrigerator, and an entire kitchen set were held together by a few bungee cords and hung precariously over the Tahoe's hood.

"Man, do you see that idiot?" Rex shouted. "He just cut me off and then slammed on his brakes!"

The Gonzalez Scrap Metal driver continued on from the stop sign at his customary fifteen miles per hour.

"Maybe that's how those foreigners drive in Uganda or wherever he's from, but we do it different here." Rex went through the stop sign and got right up on the truck's rear bumper. An arm came out of the cab, waving him around, but Rex would not budge. A police car drove by in the opposite direction, and the officer gave the Tahoe a long look.

"You know, Rex, there are a lot of guys like that around here, and they all drive the same way," Thomas said patiently.

"Oh yeah?"

"Most of them don't have insurance, either. So if you get into an accident with them, you will have to pay for the repairs yourself."

"Really?"

"Besides, you don't want to have this beautiful Tahoe in the shop for a couple weeks, do you? Better give this guy some space."

"Yeah." Rex eased back reluctantly as if his manhood had been called into question somehow.

"What did you say your name was? Carl something?"

"Thomas Clarke."

"Clarke, yeah. Do you come around here a lot?"

"I live around here. Traffic on Devon Avenue has always been slow."

"You live around here? This is like a ghetto."

"It's not that bad. You know, if you want to make better time, we can take some side streets." The junker drove on as the Tahoe came up to a red light.

"No, we're almost there." Rex looked around at the people on the street. "Thank God we don't have all these foreigners by my house. If we did, I would move in a heartbeat."

"Yeah, Rex, we could move to New York or California. There are no foreigners there," Steve added as they arrived at the Axis Testing Facility, a small storefront in a poorly constructed strip mall.

All the parking spaces in the mall were taken, so Rex shot back on the street and pulled in front of a fire hydrant. Thomas gave a look of concern, but Rex pointed to the Chicago Fire Department, Local 2 Union sticker in the front window. Rex then spit on the street and walked inside. They signed in, sat, and waited. Thomas pulled out St. Augustine again, while Rex and Steve caught up with all the celebrity gossip of the day on their cell phones.

A woman wearing a Bluetooth earpiece came out from behind a partition and paused her conversation, "Hold on a sec, dear." She looked at the three. "Okay, I am going to need the release forms from your school."

They looked at one another in confusion, then Thomas spoke. "Ma'am, we don't have any release forms. Our school nurse told us to report here for a physical."

"Nah, hon, it doesn't work that way. We need those release forms first so that we are not held liable. You have got to get those forms, hon." She turned and walked back, continuing her previous conversation.

Steve was lost. "What do we do now, Rex?"

"I don't know. I am starving."

"We need to go back and get those forms," Thomas said.

"What if the nurse doesn't even have the forms?" Rex asked, practically pouting.

"Look, the Illinois High School Association won't let us try out for football without these physicals," Thomas replied. "Let's go back, get the release forms, and make it back here before this place closes."

Steve seemed to agree, but he waited for Rex, who wanted to pout some more. Rex eventually started back to the Tahoe. As they climbed back in, Thomas took charge. He glanced at his watch. It was 4:35. "We all have other places we want to be right now. Take the streets I tell you, and we will be back at the school in no time."

Surprisingly, Rex followed Thomas's route without argument. They quickly pulled up to the school, cleared security, and rushed to the nurse's office, which was already locked. Thomas told them to wait there, and he took off running. Coming up to the principal's office as Charlene was about to leave for the evening, he called out, "Excuse me, ma'am. My name is Thomas Clarke. I was here earlier today."

"Thomas, of course, I remember you."

"Thank you, ma'am. Could you please do me a big favor?"

Charlene gladly gave Thomas three release forms and told him to leave them in the office mail slot after his physical. She would send them in to the state on Monday morning. After thanking her profusely, he ran back to the nurse's station, and despite their short attention spans, Rex and Steve were still there. Thomas waved the forms in the air, and they piled back in the Tahoe, roaring out of the parking lot once again. Ignoring Thomas's directions back to the test facility, though, Rex went right back on Devon Avenue, confidently stating, "We got time." Thomas buckled up and hoped for light traffic.

Steve turned back to Thomas and asked, "How did you get the forms?"

"I asked the secretary in the principal's office. She was very helpful."

"So you must be one of those AP students, huh?"

Thomas was shocked by Steve's observation.

"Well, yes, I am. Why would you say that?"

"They are the only ones who go there without getting yelled at. They always get stuff, too." Thomas was unsure how to take that statement, and Steve continued, "So I heard they give you guys a lot of homework. Is that true?"

Rex looked in the rearview mirror to see how Thomas would respond. When Thomas stated that, on average, their homework took about four hours a day, Rex could not believe it. "You do four hours of homework every day? That is crazy! I don't do four hours of homework in a week!"

"Well, I get an hour of study hall, and if I get into the AP/Honors Club, that will be another hour. So it's just a few hours at home every night."

Steve had never talked to someone like this before in his life. He couldn't help but ask for clarification. "You do your homework in study hall?"

"I have to. If I fell behind with my classwork, I would never be able to catch up. Why? What do you do in study hall?"

"Text usually, you know, and talk about stuff."

Thomas nodded his head.

Steve thought for a second, then continued his questions. "So you are probably going to a good college next year, huh?"

"I don't know. College is expensive. I will apply in January and see what happens. Where are you going to apply to?"

Steve did not know if he had any clothes to wear tomorrow, much less where or if he would apply to college next year. "Um. I don't know. Rex has a good chance of getting a free ride to West Idaho State, though."

Rex corrected him. "It's West Arkansas Tech, and they have been looking at me for a while. It's probably the best NAIA football program in the country, so it—whoa!" Rex slammed on the brakes.

Thomas cringed and braced for impact as he heard the squeals of tires behind him. Rex yelled out excitedly, "Squirrel fight! Dude, check it out!"

Thomas scanned the street, thinking this was some kind of secret code between Rex and Steve. Sure enough, though, two squirrels were in some kind of territorial battle and chasing each other around a tree. To see it, Rex had stopped dead in the middle of the street, almost caused three accidents, and backed up traffic for two blocks. Thomas calmly suggested they should get moving when he saw an approaching police car.

"We got time. Will you look at those squirrels? They are going to town!"

The police officer came up next to the driver's side door and announced over the loudspeaker, "You in the black Tahoe, move it along." Rex slowly drove off but only after giving the police car a look of disgust, pointing to the Local 2 Union sticker, and stating how lucky that cop was that Rex's dad was not here. Rex again pulled into the hydrant space ten minutes before closing time. "See, I told you. We have plenty of time."

They signed back in and waited. As Rex wondered aloud why the fat chick was taking so long, Steve continued to pepper Thomas with questions.

"How did you know about the physical and the forms?"

"Last year, at my old school, we made the playoffs downstate. One of our opponents made a big stink about a preseason physical for somebody on our team. Everything turned out all right, but the state officials were very thorough when they examined the records."

"Where did you play last year?"

"St. Titus. It was a small school around here."

"Didn't they win the Class 2A championship last year?"

"Yes, we did."

"Didn't they have some weird nickname?"

"We were the Cretans of St. Titus."

"That is the stupidest name I have ever heard," Rex declared confidently.

"Well, it is actually from the Bible, but the nickname was not given to the school until the 1950s. I think it was somebody's idea of a joke back then."

Steve was intrigued. "If you won state last year, you must be pretty good. What position did you play?"

"I was the quarterback, but the reason we won was because the seniors were outstanding."

"Yeah, that's all fine," Rex said. "Just so you know, Steve plays quarterback, and I play running back. He hands the ball off to me. Yeah, you won the championship, but that was Class 2A. We play Class 7A up here . . . the big time."

"So, how did you guys do last year?"

Rex and Steve hemmed and hawed as the medical tech with the earpiece came out. Looking at the clock, which read five minutes to five, she let out a long sigh and called Thomas in.

The woman was short, rotund, and in her mid-thirties. A few strands of thin, bleach blonde hair stuck out from beneath her hairnet. After taking Thomas's release form and quickly checking off at least fifty things, she grabbed another form and frantically began to make more checkmarks as she continued her phone conversation, completely ignoring Thomas.

"I don't know what Sally wants. I talked to Mary Ellen the other day, and she said Sally won't talk to her anymore. No. I know. I don't know about that." She motioned Thomas over to check his blood pressure. "So I think we should all go out for drinks and just clear the air. Yes, don't you love that place? Oh, I have been unbelievably busy today. It's been unreal. Any who, I told Mary Ellen."

She took Thomas's height and weight and did more checking on the form. "Because, you know, right now, I am hungry like the wolf. Oh, I love that song! That is one of my favorite songs of all time. What ever happened to Duran Duran? I know, you always loved Simon, but John Taylor was my favorite. He was so cute. . . . " She made a few more checks on the form, and Thomas was finished.

Ten minutes later, Rex and Steve were done as well. As they came back to the Tahoe, there was a $150 ticket on the windshield for blocking the hydrant.

"What? Is that cop blind? The sticker is right there. Wait until my dad finds out about this."

Rex flew out of the hydrant space and did a quick U-turn to get back to school. Coming up to a red light, Rex watched a group of older men in black suits talking on the corner.

"Man, it is nothing but Jews and foreigners around here. I don't even know where all these Arabs come from."

"Actually, they are mostly Pakistani and Indian, not Arabs," Thomas replied.

"Whatever. Jews, Arabs. They all come from one of those countries where everyone is stupid. Look at this guy here. He doesn't even know how to park."

Rex gave the minivan in front of him a two-second grace period before he sped into oncoming traffic to get around him, stating emphatically, "We should have finished them all off when we fought that war."

Thomas was intrigued by that statement and inquired, "What war was that, Rex?"

"You know, that war like twenty-five or thirty years ago in Southeast Arabia."

"That war twenty-five years ago in Southeast Arabia? No, I don't know that one, Rex."

"You don't remember that? Steve, you know what I am talking about, right?"

"Yeah, I think so, Rex. That war, right?"

"Yeah. Well, I guess Professor Brainiac isn't that smart after all. It was that war when the Jews and Arabs invaded some place, an island I think it was. So we went in there and kicked their ass." He gave Steve a high five before continuing, "But the Russians or the European government or somebody said we had to stop. Then we had to let all these Jews and Arabs come here. That's how 9/11 happened."

Thomas was going to respond, but he let it pass. He figured he would just be wasting his breath.

"What now?" Rex saw the flashing hazard lights of a silver Chevy Suburban five cars ahead. A slender, balding Middle Eastern man got out. He was dressed in brown sandals, dark brown polyester pants, and a brown-and-white–striped polyester shirt buttoned halfway up. As the man adjusted the gold chains around his neck and then his gigantic gold watch, Rex laid on the horn. In the oncoming traffic lane, a bus stopped right next to the Tahoe, and Rex was pinned in.

"Steve, get up there and get that foreigner to move his car!" Rex barked.

"You got it, boss." Steve flew out of the Tahoe and sprinted up to the Suburban. "Hey, you can't park that here. You have to move that thing."

Looking over Steve very deliberately, the man gave a big grin, hunched his shoulders, put out his hands, and said in a thick accent, "Come on, buddy. Don't be like that, buddy."

"Buddy? I am not your buddy! You have to move that car!"

The man slowly started to move toward the curb and kept smiling as he said, "Hey, buddy. Come on. You see the blinkers. You know."

"Move that piece of crap now!" Steve insisted.

"Come on, buddy. The blinkers mean you can park anywhere you want. You know that, buddy. Come on. Don't be like that."

"Listen, you stupid foreigner, move the car!"

"Hey, you see the blinkers, buddy. I have the blinkers on. You know. Come on. Don't be like that, buddy."

The man walked down the street a few feet and disappeared into a store. Rex was about to jump out of the driver's seat, but Thomas stopped him and said, "Rex, let me have your and Steve's paperwork. I'll bring it back to the school, and you won't have to worry about going back." Rex tossed the papers over his shoulder and raced up to Steve.

Thomas collected what he needed and made his way back to the school on foot as the security guards were locking things down for the weekend. He cleared security again and dropped the forms at the principal's office. He checked the time. Five twenty-five. He would have to hurry home to eat before going to work with his dad, and then in four or five hours, he could finally rest.

CHAPTER 7

"I don't care how well the Cubs did all season or what their record is; this nosedive to start September is more indicative of the real team," Richard said to no one in particular.

"McGee, what is your problem? Do you know what is happening? The country is on the brink of financial collapse. Don't you even care?" Scott Weber was becoming unglued. He was surrounded by a group of students frantically devouring the latest financial news on their cell phones and PDAs. Richard ignored him and moved over to another homeroom seat, but he still remained close enough to the irate Scott Weber and the others.

"Look, their starting pitching is okay. Dempster, Lilly, and Zambrano are decent. Their position players, though, are all overachievers. Pinella sprinkled some kind of magic dust over them during the regular season, but it's not going to last. Derrick Lee is solid, and so is Edmonds, but he is about fifty-two years old. They just don't have the horses to make a long run in the playoffs."

"Are you completely insane? Look at this!" Scott shoved his Blackberry in Richard's face. "We are going to have another Great Depression, and you are talking about sports. Any day now, instead of preparing for medical school, I could be in a soupline, with God only knows who, maybe for the next ten or twenty years! Do you even know how much I enjoy going to my family's summerhouse?"

"Forget about the Cubs. Forget about the Bears. Nobody pays any attention to hockey, so you might as well wait for the Bulls. They have a hardworking team, and Rose could turn out to be a good draft pick," Richard again said to no one in particular.

With a devilish grin, Richard came over to where Thomas and Marie were sitting quietly. Scott kept his distance and paced the room with his nose buried in his phone, pausing only occasionally to let out sighs of desperation.

"For some reason, they think I know about everything that happens in the government," Richard said.

"How did they ever get that idea, Rich?" Thomas replied with a smile.

"I don't know, but Scotty Boy is all whipped into a lather and is assuming the worst. Why aren't you two in the throes of despair as well?"

"Irrational fear achieves nothing. To be fair, though, I do not understand all the financial matters that are being talked about in the news, but the reporters are using a much more dire tone to describe these events. The problem is serious," Thomas said. Marie sat quietly and listened intently.

"Yes, probably. Look at what is being said, though. The government financial experts and the Federal Reserve guys are saying that the entire banking system is going to vaporize at any second, and they claim that our whole economy will follow right behind it. The news media is hyping up all the talk of an immediate apocalypse, suggesting that we can't wait even until the end of today to take drastic action. Something has to be done instantaneously, right?"

"From what I have heard, that is accurate," Thomas replied.

Richard continued, "The Congress, meanwhile, has said in return, let's hold some hearings, and we'll get back to you in a month or so. Come on. This I do know about government types: you can't take anything they say at face value. Every word out of their mouth is spin—for the party, for a caucus, or for themselves. It's all scripted to suit a certain purpose. I don't understand the financial stuff either, but I am sure that whatever you are seeing in the media, the actual truth of the matter is something quite different."

"We know you are holding back on us, McGee," Scott said. Scott had succeeded in convincing a good number of others that the nation would not survive to the end of homeroom. They were terrified and wanted answers now.

"When people are this worked up, it's like shooting fish in a barrel," Richard said quietly to Thomas and Marie.

"All right, Scott," Richard relented, appearing deadly serious as he came over and looked each member of Scott Weber's hysterical cabal in the eye. "I am going to tell you all something that none of you can repeat to anyone ever. Okay?" They all agreed. Richard looked as if he was uncertain about continuing, but then he pulled them in closer. "I should not be telling you this, and if anyone asks, I will deny it. No, I can't do this."

Richard tried to pull away from the pack, but Scott exploded, "Come on, McGee!"

Richard reluctantly returned. He gathered them all back in and said, "There has been a plan in place for some time now. What you see now is just the opening move. For your own safety, I can't give you all the details. I can tell you one word, though: Amero." That set off a flurry of Internet searches, and Richard looked around the room furtively. "The United States, Mexico, and Canada will unite into one country, and the Amero will be the new currency. You may have heard something about this already, but what you don't know is this: the Amero currency will not be based on any standard of gold or silver. Instead, the standard will be based on neon tetras."

"The fish?"

"Yes, the fish. They are very rare," Richard said dismissively as the Amero information poured into their cell phones. "My family and some others have been hoarding neon tetras for some time now. Here's the thing, though. My family has the precious three-stripe tetras, while everyone else has the common four-stripers. So none of us need to worry. Everyone at this school will be taken care of as long as you all are ready to defend my family's stockpile of three-stripe neon tetras with your lives. It could get ugly when the word gets out." That statement caused some serious soul searching in the group. "The other thing you don't know is that the Grand Field Marshall of the Royal Canadian Mounted Police is going to be our new Supreme Overlord at least temporarily. We only have a short time now until it is all accomplished."

Some members of the crowd around Richard were skeptical, but most were stunned because the Internet information backed up some of his statements. Even though Richard let them all off the hook by the end of the day, it took a few weeks for some to be totally convinced that he was kidding.

Coming up to Thomas and Marie, he said, "See what people will believe when they are afraid?"

"How do you say those things with a straight face? I could never do it," Thomas said.

"Neither could I," Marie added. "Although isn't the proper question, why do you say those things?"

"It's difficult sometimes. I suppose it is a gift."

"If you would only use your powers for good," Thomas said.

Almost out of breath, Scott came up to Richard with a few questions about an Amero rumor he had found on the Web, but Principal Diaz's voice came across the loudspeaker.

"Ladies and gentlemen, good morning. I am sorry for the interruption, but I have a sad announcement. Mr. Geoffrey Spencer died suddenly last night. He had been a teacher in the Chicago Public Schools for twenty-six years, the last three as an English instructor at West Ridge Preparatory Academy. All of our thoughts should be with his family and loved ones. Grief counselors will be made available to anyone who requires their services. Thank you."

Marie sat quietly, watching.

"Wow! He was a good guy," Richard said, clearly sobered by the news. "Tom, didn't you tell me he was in the same class at St. Titus as your dad?"

"No, he was the year behind my dad."

Richard sat quietly, pondering the fact that John Clarke was four years younger than Charles McGee.

***

"This is great stuff, Mr. Clarke," the principal said.

"Thank you, sir."

As part of the administration's response to the death of a student or faculty member, all the students are required to write a paper describing their feelings, and Dr. Diaz was deep into Thomas's two-page exposition on death.

"'Brief as the life of a flower, the short span of our miserable precarious existence is rushing past; and meanwhile we drink, and call for garlands, perfumes, and girls, and old age steals upon us unperceived.' Who is the guy that said that? Goo-ven somebody?"

"Juvenal, sir. He was a Roman satirist."

"And this one, 'It is certain that we must die, what is uncertain is whether it will be today.' That was a guy named Cicero, huh?"

"Yes, sir."

"You know, there is a suburb west of Chicago called Cicero. I wonder if the two are related somehow?"

"I believe they are, sir."

"Then this ending here, where you say that a peaceful mind is unaffected by clouds and thunder, and it will stand safely on the shore while others are shipwrecked. That's fantastic stuff."

"Thank you, sir. That was a paraphrase of Petrarch, an Italian poet," Thomas replied, trying to mask his displeasure. "Sir, there is nothing original in anything that I wrote, so I can't take credit for it. I used those statements because I believe they are true and that they needed to be said. I quoted those authors because they could speak more clearly and precisely than I, not to show that I can memorize some sayings or to make myself look good."

"Nonsense! This is great. It's not as good as your AP/Honors Club application speech, but look at what some of these other papers say. 'I am sad,' or 'I am sorry he died.' I want to put your words in the next edition of the school paper and also submit them to the citywide newsletter that every school administrator receives, with your permission, of course."

"If you wish, sir."

"Great. Keep up the good work."

Ricardo Diaz's mind was spinning, and he began to sweat. The weather had cooled from the sweltering heat and humidity of August, but Dr. Diaz could sweat in a blizzard while conjuring up in his mind the machinations of his future career. He dismissed Thomas and mentioned that a permanent replacement for Mr. Spencer had been found.

CHAPTER 8

Margaret Clarke pulled up and parked under the shade of a tree in front of Clarke Printing. She saw her husband gazing up at the branches. An item in the newspaper stated that Dutch elm disease had been spotted in the area and that it could be spread by the elm bark beetle. John was on a futile hunt and said to his wife, "I can't tell if that little bug is in this tree. The leaves are wilting, but is that because of autumn or because of this fungus? I guess we won't know until next spring . . . if we are even here next spring."

Margaret followed him inside and looked around for the box she was going to deliver. The local newspapers were open on the desk, and the computer screen displayed two more news sites. Government officials, bankers, CEOs, and the experts in the media were all blaring an unrelenting, morose call of financial destruction. Margaret read it all intently and then asked where the posters were. She had a student arriving for a piano lesson in an hour. There was enough time for her to make this delivery, run to the store, and pick up Kathleen from school.

John brought in the brightly colored signs announcing a weekend farmers market on the St. Aloysius University campus. Looking over the information, it dawned on Margaret that she herself had reaped the bounty of the earth. She would have to find out if it was possible for her to sell some of her produce. The spot chosen for the market was an empty lot were an old dormitory had stood. It was just a cleared-off concrete slab, but it was adjacent to the lake where massive boulders had been placed to act as an artificial breakwater. Jutting out from them were the worn wooden pylons of an ancient pier that now served as a place of rest for seagulls, tired from their fishing in the shallows. Margaret often took early walks by that spot, and she always found it to be a rare oasis of peace and quiet in the bustling city. The morning sun would always struggle to reach across the vast, rippling expanse of the water's blue-green surface and then softly bathe the maroon and cream art deco university buildings in light. Even at this late date in the year, white sails dotted the dark canvas of the lake and skimmed along slowly and serenely, enjoying the last of the smooth, warm air. *The farmers market will be a lovely way to spend a few hours on a Saturday morning,* she thought.

Margaret gave the news one last, quick look before putting her arm around her husband's shoulders. He saw the way she was looking at him, and he said to her, "We certainly do live in the United States of Hyperbole, don't we?"

She kissed her husband and went on her way. A few minutes later, the front doorbell rang, and John came out to meet Bob Einhart.

"Bob, thanks for coming. Please come on in and have a seat. How are you?" John showed him into the office.

"Retirement agrees with me, John."

"That's good to hear. How are Helen and the boys?"

"The boys are all out of college and trying to find any position they can to justify all the money I just shelled out for their tuition. Helen, I am afraid, has been driven completely insane with me being at home all the time now."

An electrician by trade, Bob Einhart was tall and heavyset, with powerful forearms and the stomach of a beer drinker. Over his short, gray and light brown hair, he always affixed a worn-out baseball hat. It was impossible to read whatever logo may have been on it at one time. An unbuttoned flannel shirt with the sleeves rolled up covered a white T-shirt, and the tattered hem of beat-up blue jeans were loosely tucked into the top of grime-encrusted work boots. He had been brought up with a German work ethic and a desire for precision. Despite the gruff exterior, he was a kind man and very generous with his time, having worked many side jobs for fellow St. Titus parishioners, including the Clarke family. Electrical work is not what John needed today, though. Bob had just retired after twenty-six years as a building inspector for the City of Chicago.

After reading over the violation letter and examining the exterior and rear door of Clarke Printing, Bob got a disgusted look on his face. "You see this number here. This identifies who the inspector is. This is the son of a union boss who is heavy with the fifth floor at city hall. The kid never went to any trade school and doesn't know anything. From what I have seen, your building is fine. Let me give you the number of a supervisor who can clear this up. Tell the guy who answers that I told you to call."

"That is great, Bob. Thanks a million."

"Ah, it's nothing. I am sorry you had to deal with this headache."

"Well, actually, there is something else I would like you to look at. I received this a few days ago. You know that I am willing to do what I need to do to keep this place safe. I don't want to work in a dangerous building, but this seems excessive."

He handed Bob an envelope that featured a Chicago Fire Department logo on it. Bob raised his eyebrows more than a few times as he read the letter. Then he read the identifying number of the fire inspector and sighed.

"Yeah," Bob said while rubbing his hand on his face. "Can we take a look inside?"

A five-minute walk was all that was needed, and they came back to the office.

"Is someone upset with you for some reason?" Bob asked jokingly. "Look, all of this is just ridiculous. I know this inspector, too. She is saying here that you need to have an EPA document certifying that your floor drain meets the federal standards for the disposal of hazardous waste. That's crazy. She is only supposed to enforce the city's fire codes, and your floor drain has nothing to do with fire safety or hazardous waste. You don't have any hazardous waste here at all. You don't have to get that certificate."

"Are you sure? Because I looked into that, and it would cost $20,000 to have the EPA come here, dig up my floor, and do their tests. They would have to shut down my business for two weeks while they were working, too. That is great news! Are you 100 percent certain?"

"Yes, John. She had no reason to write that apart from the fact that she is a complete nitwit. The city has no authority to write federal EPA violations, but that woman feels she can make up any law she wants to and force people to comply with it. Now, for this other stuff, you don't need to build a flammable liquid room. You have acetone, which is a Class I flammable liquid, but you use and store much less than ten gallons on the premises. After twenty years as fire inspector, that simpleton should have known that." It was clear from his tone that Bob was getting upset.

"Fantastic! That was going to be another $15,000," John replied with relief.

"Now, about this hazardous material license . . . " Bob paused and grimaced. "You store and use less than thirty gallons, so by law you are not required to have a license. However, I have heard from some reliable people that the mayor told the commissioner of revenue that the city needs money. The revenue people have been going out and forcing business owners to buy licenses that they are not legally required to have."

"What?"

"They will throw you in court, fine you big money, and threaten to take away your business license. They will essentially shut you down unless you cough up some money."

"There was a revenue guy here yesterday who said those exact words. He wants me to buy a two-year hazardous material license for $2,500. He also told me I had to pay a $350 fine for not having the license already. If I hear you right, that's extortion. How do they expect anyone to be able to earn a living? It's hard enough for businesses operating here already; I can't see how any new business could possibly open up. Don't the city officials want there to be jobs here anymore? It seems like they only want more condos."

Twenty-six years of frustration bubbled up and out of Bob Einhart. "A lot of people who work for the city simply don't care how city policies affect you. I can't tell you how many people I have worked with that think if someone owns his or her own business, then that person must have a pile of money sitting in a room somewhere. So what if it costs you $20,000 to fix something? You own your own business, and you are a millionaire. That is honestly how they think."

"I can tell you that is not true at all. My business has dropped off to almost nothing, and everyone else I talk to says the same thing. Gloom and doom is everywhere you go."

"I'll tell you, John, when I started with the city, there were some shenanigans going on, but most workers there, including the supervisors, knew how to do their jobs. In the last few years, though, it has gotten out of control. There are a lot of people in positions of authority now who should not be in charge of anything except maybe mopping a floor. You just can't make people the bosses who are not capable of handling the jobs they oversee. They screw up all sorts of things, but the city big shots don't care because they know there are a handful of people in every department who know what they are doing and will clean up the damn mess and make things work. I could have stayed a few more years and maxed out my pension, but I had had it up to here. The day I left was one of the greatest days of my life." Bob's face was getting red.

"Jeez, Bob, I did not mean for you to get upset. I'm sorry."

"No, no, no. It's fine. John, you know how frustrating it can be dealing with the city bureaucracy once in a while. You can imagine how frustrating it was to work every day in that insane asylum with its institutionalized inefficiency and mediocrity. I don't have to deal with that stuff anymore, and I shouldn't let it get to me. You know, I worked in the private sector for eighteen years before I started with the city, and there, you had to know your stuff. I drove all over creation just to get to the job site, and then I worked my behind off all day. If I didn't, I would have been let go. It just frosts my shorts when I see the city crush honest, hardworking guys like you. You're just trying to earn a living, yet they burden you with excessive taxes, fees, and license requirements. And then they just flush that money down the toilet on some lazy, good-for-nothing bum or some stupid new program. You know, that half-brain Lt. Travers is a supervisor and makes $120,000 a year."

"Holy cow!" John blurted out. He was shocked to hear that, especially since he and George had recently taken a 15 percent pay cut. "Bob, is there anything I can do about this room and the license?"

"Well, for the room and the drain, you can call up the fire inspector's office and start asking questions. I can show you where to get the correct information regarding your alleged violations on the Internet. Like I said, they do have some decent people there. Chances are that the person you talk with will be overwhelmed with your questions and will try to transfer you to someone else. Just be persistent, and that should take care of that. For the license, I would fight it if I were you. The city takes enough of your money. I can show you also where to get the information you will need to beat them."

"Well, is there any way you could come along and help me at the hearing?"

"I wish I could, but no. Every year I had to sign an ethics statement that forbids retired city employees from helping a party sue the city or helping a party defend themselves from city action. They could mess with my pension if I did. I am sorry."

"Bob, I understand. I appreciate everything you've done. You have potentially saved me $35,000 that, to be honest, I don't have. I have a big pile of other expenses, which I don't have money for either, that I can now try to figure out how I am going to pay for. I can't thank you enough."

"Glad to help. I hope things pick up for you, John." Bob noticed but did not mention how tired and stressed out John appeared. "It's good to see that you are still hanging in there. Driving down the street is depressing. So many people are going out of business. Is that what happened next door here?"

"Actually, the guy who was next door is doing great. He has a machine shop that makes some special parts for a tank and a helicopter. Orders from the military have kept him going strong. Fortunately for him, he got a nice tax deal from one of the suburbs and moved out there. He is a good man. I am glad things are going well for him. On the other side, Hans Volker is a woodworker. He was an incredible artist, but he is seventy-five years old. The last time I saw him use his shop was a few years ago when he made two violins for his granddaughters. Now his building sits mostly empty. Since this place to the north sold, the creepy developer who bought it has been coming around here looking at this building, too."

"John, did I see correctly that the developer was Silver Screen Realty?"

"Yes, that's them."

"Silver Screen Realty and Development is owned by the son-in-law of our illustrious alderman Stein."

"That would explain quite a bit."

"There are a lot of shady things going on with that group, John. Be careful."

"I will. Thanks for everything, Bob."

CHAPTER 9

Offensive tackle Jeff Loder came up to the backs and the receivers, who were stretching out. Jeff asked, "Hey, Clarke, did I hear somebody say you went to St. Titus last year?"

"Yes, I did."

"Did you go there for grammar school, too?"

"Yes."

"I'm from St. Martin of Tours. We used to play you guys."

"Oh, yes, I remember. There were some St. Martin alumni who played at St. Ti's last year. They were good players."

"Well, we always had a decent team, but there were three guys the year ahead of us at St. Titus that always killed us. Man, they were great. Who were those guys?"

"Burke, Brandonisio, and Walsh. Yeah, they were tough. Last year, Walsh was an all-state running back; Brandonisio was all-state linebacker; and Burke was an all-state and all-American offensive tackle. It was really a fluke for such a small school to have three outstanding players like that."

"Those guys would kick my butt from the opening kickoff until the last whistle. There was never any let up in them."

"They were full throttle in every drill in practice, too."

"Is that where you got it from?"

Thomas had earned Jeff Loder's respect on the first day of practice. During a pursuit and downfield tackling drill, Loder got an angle on Thomas, who was carrying the ball and racing for the sidelines. Instead of running out of bounds to avoid being hit by the six-foot-three, 230-pound lineman, Thomas slowed as if he was going to cut back and get behind the tackler. When Loder slowed to prevent this, Thomas now had the advantage in momentum and exploded at full speed into the chest of his surprised adversary. Loder reeled from the force of the impact and was driven back three yards, struggling to keep his grip. Thomas went down eventually, but Loder got up shaking out some cobwebs.

"Even though I was the quarterback, they were the senior captains. They set the tone. They would have kicked my butt and anyone else's on the team, too, if any of us slacked off. That's what good leaders do. The coaches taught us the right way to play and worked all of us hard. It paid off in the end."

"I guess that's what makes a champion. A little different from what we have this year, huh?"

"Yes, but there is nothing I can do about the coaches here or how they run a team. Rex was named the captain, and that's that. No matter what anyone else does, though, I control how hard I practice and how hard I play in the games."

"Yeah." Loder thought about that for a second. "Say, whatever happened to those three guys?"

"Walsh received a scholarship to Northern Illinois; Brandonisio was awarded a scholarship to St. Norbert's; and Burke got a full ride to Iowa."

"No kidding? That's pretty cool." Loder shook his head. Then he asked, "Hey, man, you want to smoke a doob before practice?"

Thomas declined as the head coach and his staff walked up. Coach Green never paid much attention to his players. He felt very strongly that he had paid his dues, toiling away for two decades as a seventh-grade math teacher to subsidize his true calling of being a football coach. Now it was his turn. A real budget, a real staff, and no pressure to win. Who says the life of a sycophant doesn't pay off eventually? West Ridge was an egghead school, so no one expected them to compete in athletics. After three seasons and no wins, the only warning given to him by the school administration was to make certain that there were no injuries.

The parents, on the other hand, could be draining if he let them be. The constant badgering about everything from more playing time for their untalented kids, to what colors the uniforms should be, to play calling suggestions could wear a coach down at a competitive school, but not here. They could complain as much as they wanted. Coach Green's life and career were on cruise control. No worries. Practice didn't even start until a week after the other schools did. After a few more years of riding this gravy train, he could retire with his full pension.

The West Ridge outdoor practice facilities, to the north of the school, were expansive. The football, soccer, and baseball practice fields lined up successively, with the river bordering east and a thick blanket of trees surrounding the other sides. The upcoming season opener would be this Friday night in the main stadium to the south of the campus.

There were a few decent players that could make it at a real program, and the team would be prepared as best as he was willing. Win or lose, his checks came either way. Nothing was going to break the coach's serenity. Fortune had been kind to him, but fortune can change quickly.

Coach Green's heart began to palpitate when he heard an approaching siren. He went into mild apoplexy as a fire engine jumped the curb, lights flashing, and began to make its way through the trees and across the baseball and soccer fields. It was headed right toward him. He blew his whistle and quickly told the team that practice would begin in ten minutes as he and the staff made a hasty retreat out of sight.

Thomas could not see any smoke at the school and wondered if someone had gotten hurt. The blaring siren pounded his ears, and a man hanging out the front passenger window was pulling something that set off an air horn. The engine sped up, then skidded to a stop, tearing up the recently sodded turf.

The team stood watching as a firefighter in a white shirt jumped out. He yelled excitedly in a gravelly Chicago accent, "There he is! There he is! There's my boy! There's the king!"

"Dad, what are you doing here?" Rex said.

"Hey, Mr. Burger," Steve added.

Lt. Stanley Burger waddled up with one hand rubbing the bushy, dyed-black mustache on his chubby face. He said, "That's my boy. That's the king. We named him Rex because he is the king at whatever he does. Hey, Steve."

"Dad, that's Engine 146. That firehouse is like eight miles from here. Aren't you way out of your still area?"

"Hey, if they want to get pimpy about me wanting to see my boy to wish him good luck before his big game, go right ahead. Besides, they can get me if they need me." Lt. Burger pointed with his disproportionally small arms to the radio strapped across his expansive stomach and the well-entrenched food stains across the front of the shirt.

"Dad, did Mom tell you that I need some gas money for the Tahoe?"

"Rex, I just gave you a bunch of money last week."

"I know. I lost it over the weekend. I took Ohio State and the points, and Stanford and the over."

"Straight up? Oh, Rexy. You have to parlay that stuff. What were you thinking?"

"Dad, I told you not to call me that in public. Besides, Ohio State and Stanford were due. Come on, just give me a hundred. Come on." Rex started to whine, and his father quickly gave in.

"Hey, you are my boy, my only man-child. I can't say no to you." After handing over the money, Lt. Burger grabbed his son's jersey and said, "But don't you think for one second that your old man still can't take you."

Rex deflected the attempted headlock, and the two briefly struggled like sumo wrestlers, arms flailing. Lt. Burger retreated momentarily, then made a bull rush at Rex, who sidestepped, lost his balance, and took hold of his father up near the shoulder. Momentum flipped them both over, with Lt. Burger crashing down on the wet grass underneath Rex. His and his son's full ample weight knocked the wind completely out of him. Stan Burger let out a moan as waves of intense pain surged through his body. Struggling in futility to arise, his face flushed and then turned ashen, and he went back down.

"Oh my God! I think my spleen ruptured," he said, gasping for air.

"Dad, are you okay?" Rex asked, trying to get his father on his feet. He looked over at the young firefighters, who had never strayed from the engine, as if they should do something, but they remained impassively in place.

Stan Burger waved off Rex and stayed on his back, writhing on the ground until his breath returned. He eventually got to one knee and said, "I'm all right. I'm all right."

Rex went over to try and wipe off the large grass stain on the back of his father's soaking wet uniform shirt and to look for the buttons that had flown off. "Oh no! Your shirt is ripped up, and your radio is broken. Won't you get in trouble for that?"

"Hey, listen," the elder Burger replied, bent over and panting, his anger rising, "I risked my life every day on this job for twenty-seven years. I almost died on this job more than once. If they want to ding me for something like that . . . " As huge purple veins bulged from his temples and neck, he pointed at the broken $1,800 radio without finishing his thought.

"Hey, Lieutenant, they are calling us," one of the firefighters announced.

"Huh?"

"The main fire alarm office is calling. They want to know why we are here. The battalion chief and the district chief are on their way."

CHAPTER 10

"So, have you heard anything about our new English teacher, Thomas?" Marie asked.

"Nothing really. Richard heard that he is coming from a small private school on the east coast. We shall find out more later this afternoon."

Thomas put his books in his locker and grabbed his lunch. He and Marie headed toward the cafeteria. They turned a corner and saw William Donohue trying to pick up his books, which were scattered all over the hallway. Rex was standing over him, stating defiantly, "You've got to watch where you are going, Donohue."

William thanked Rex for his very prudent advice as he calmly and methodically picked up his books in precise, preferred order: thickest to thinnest and then alphabetized by subject and author. Thomas walked up, with Marie behind him, and asked William if everything was all right.

"Oh, most definitely. Thank you."

"Yeah, Donohue just needs to be more careful," Rex repeated before going on his way.

Thomas helped William up and asked again, "Are you all right, William?"

"Of course. It was nothing. I believe we are all presently scheduled to be in the cafeteria. Shall we be on our way?" There was no agitation in William's voice, so Thomas let it drop.

Thomas and Marie both brought their lunches and found a table. William got in line ahead of Richard, who had just horrified and amused some freshmen by telling them that eating too many grapes at once can cause violent diarrhea. Richard further entertained them with the story a girl he knew, who had been given a Novocain shot in her abdomen to dull the area from pain when receiving a belly button piercing. The unlicensed gentleman performing the piercing stuck the needle in too far. Her intestines, bowels, and bladder were all numbed by the drug, and she lost control of her bodily functions. She became so dehydrated that paramedics had to come and save her life. Richard admonished the youngsters against trying to be cool with a body piercing. The freshmen thought it was both the most revolting and the greatest story they had ever heard.

"You look tired. Do you feel all right, Thomas?" Marie inquired.

"I have had to work a few nights this week with my dad. Business has been so slow recently. When he gets a big order, which is rare, I don't want to turn him down when he asks for help. I only have to go in for an hour or so tonight. Then I will have Friday night free for the game. Oh, Marie, that reminds me," he paused abruptly. She could tell it was not going to be good news. "Because it is the first game, we have to go over a bunch of things beforehand, and I am not going to be able to be at the AP/Honors Club on Friday for your piano recital. I am very sorry." She was disappointed, so he tried to soften the blow. "Marie, I was thinking. . . . On Sunday nights, I always have a few free hours. If you are willing, maybe you can come by our house and visit. If you would like, you can play that piano piece you have rehearsed."

"That would be wonderful." The enthusiasm of her reply made Thomas suddenly realize that this invitation was long overdue. It was very inconsiderate of him not to have thought of it earlier. She would not hear it when he tried to apologize, but he pressed on about something else that had been bothering him.

"Marie, after you moved away, I never called you once. I'm sorry."

The sudden seriousness was surprising. "I never called you either, Thomas. I should apologize as well."

"It's not like I didn't want to. You did not move all that far away, but I just got caught up in other things. I can't explain it, nor do I have any real excuse."

Marie smiled before replying, "Isn't it strange how quickly life goes by and how less important things push aside more important things?" They both vowed to never let that happen again. Thomas tried to break the somber mood by observing that if they had smartphones like everyone else, they could have texted nonstop for three years straight.

"My mother did give me one for emergencies," Marie noted, "but I usually don't take it with me. Between work, school, and home, I am always close by."

"I don't have one either, and I don't want one, but I can see where it would be useful in an emergency."

"What's going on here?" Richard plopped himself down.

This should be an interesting topic, Thomas thought. "We were just talking about smartphones and PDAs. Many people have them, but neither of us do."

Richard squinted his eyes and looked back and forth between the two. "That's because you two aren't idiots."

Thomas laughed and replied, "What do you mean?"

"Look, the people who sell and market these phones are extremely effective at what they do. They can convince almost anyone to spend a whole lot of money on a hunk of junk that they really don't need. They are masters at it, and all these sheep just do whatever they are told to do. You two have the audacity to question whether you actually need a $400 cell phone or not. Just look at these goofs over here." Richard thrust his thumb toward another table. The students he had gestured toward were staring earnestly at their cell phone screens and frantically texting. They weren't eating or conversing with one another. Richard continued, "What kind of pressing business do you think they are working on? Peace in the Middle East? They are nothing but sheep."

"Is there a hint of admiration in your voice?" Thomas asked.

"Look, the people in marketing and advertising have an almost diabolical power over the masses. If the tobacco companies, with incredible restrictions on where and how they can advertise, are still able to convince some people that they should inhale the smoke from an incredibly expensive, carcinogenic smoldering weed hanging from their lip, then people can be convinced to do just about anything. You have to give credit where credit is due." William joined them at the table. "Hey, Big Bill, do you have a cell phone?" Richard asked.

"I have one, but I rarely find an occasion for its need."

"See, there you go. Bill Donohue thinks for himself." Richard eyed the end of the table where Scott Weber had just sat down and was engrossed in the screen of his phone. Richard raised his voice and ranted, "Besides, what kind of man squawks on a phone and texts? A twelve-year-old girl maybe but not a man. All these little electronic devices are just so womanly. In fact, there are few things as emasculating as seeing a grown man play with some plastic toy. Put down the Barbie doll, Sally, and go chop some wood, for crying out loud."

Scott quietly shut down his phone and shot daggers at Richard, who smiled back and asked, "How is the soup today, Scotty?"

"Why don't you shut up, McGee?"

Richard kept smiling as he motioned Thomas and Marie in closer, "I learned some information about Dr. Diaz you might be interested in."

"What's that?"

"I got it from a good source that the superintendent of schools is going to resign at the end of this school year. Rick Diaz and the principal of Dunning Academy are the two main candidates to replace him. So Diaz has been calling up the mayor's office and a bunch of Hispanic political groups trying to kiss butt and drum up support for himself. Supposedly, he was telling them about a refugee from the Catholic schools that was going to put him over the top. Who do you think that is? Huh, Thomas, huh?"

"Wonderful," Thomas said flatly.

"However, he does not like that you are playing football, and he has you pegged for some kind of rabble-rouser that might muck up his chances. That's why he is keeping a very close eye on you." Thomas was not happy to hear that.

"Principal Diaz is only concerned with what is best for the school and for the well-being of the students," Scott fired into the conversation from down the table. "We all know about you and your inside information, McGee."

"You're not still sore about that Amero thing, are you? I apologized. Let it go."

"Nobody cares about your Springfield political gossip," Scott snorted.

"I got that right from Charlene actually."

"Charlene? Dr. Diaz's secretary? When I first met her, I feared that she was a bit mean-spirited, but she is actually very kind and helpful," Thomas said.

"Oh, she is a peach of a girl once you get to know her, and she is a big fan of yours, Tommy Boy." Richard directed his next remarks toward the other end of the table. "People appreciate it when you say 'please' and 'thank you,' sit up straight, and dress nice. Well, you don't exactly dress nice, Tom, but at least you don't dress like an inconsiderate slob. The point is, if you are nice to her, she will be nice to you."

"Some people take being nice for weakness," Scott interjected.

Richard fired back, "Thanks, Tony Soprano. Michael Corleone just called. Moe Green is giving him trouble out in Vegas. He wants you to get back to him as soon as possible."

"Who are they, McGee, your father's campaign finance committee?"

The venom in Scott's words sent Richard out of his seat and into one directly across from Scott. Thomas jumped up to prevent any violence, but Richard masked his anger and calmly said everything was fine. He leaned in and rubbed his chin, looking directly at Scott, who scowled back defiantly. Richard looked over Scott's shoulder until he made eye contact with a group of sophomore girls sitting at the next table.

"That's her, isn't it, Scotty?"

"What?" Scott was caught completely off guard.

"That's her, right? The one you were talking about."

"I don't know . . . what. . . . What are you saying?" Scott was clearly flustered.

"She's right there. That's the one, right?" Richard smiled and waved over to the girls.

"Will you lower you voice, please, McGee?"

"Look, she's right there. Just go ask her."

Scott Weber's face became beet red as he glanced over his shoulder at a group of giggling young girls he had never seen before.

"Just ask her. Go talk to her. She'll understand. She's right there. Go ahead."

Scott was close to total panic, putting his hands up to block his face. "Will you shut up?"

"I don't know why you just won't ask her. She's right there. I'm telling you, she'll understand."

Scott's eyes darted frantically, then he gathered his things and left in a hurry. Richard gave a wink to the girls as he slid back down the table to disapproving looks. "What? That little brownnose has to learn to stay out of other people's business. You mess with the bull, and you get the horns."

"What is it between you two?" Thomas asked.

"What do you care? He hates you, too. Marie, didn't Scott try to keep Thomas out of the AP/Honors Club?"

"Scott was very vocal about not letting Thomas in, obviously to no avail, though," Marie replied. Turning to Thomas, she added, "He did not like the religious references in your speech."

"Really? I purposely did not mention the theological virtues, and they are more important than the cardinal virtues," Thomas said innocently.

"Yeah, well, I really wish you had mentioned them because Scotty's head would have exploded." Richard could not hide his rage anymore. "He tried to keep you out of AP/Honors the same way he railroaded me out of that club!"

"Is that what this is about?"

"That's the day he moved up to the top of my list."

Susan Donohue quietly came up and sat next to her brother William, who joined the conversation by stating, "To be fair, Richard, many people, including some at this table, were offended by the confrontational tone of your speech. Most were willing to overlook that and focus on the structure of the presentation itself, which was superb. Be that as it may, it is true that Scott was pivotal in convincing many to deny your admittance."

"Listen, Billy, if you—" Richard spun around to continue his argument, then he saw Susan Donohue.

She smiled at him and softly said, "Hello."

Richard lost his train of thought and could only stammer out, "Um, hi, Susan. Uh, you look really nice." It suddenly became uncomfortably warm for Richard, who straightened his collar and fought to keep his composure. He reminded himself, *Steady on, man. Get control.* Pausing to take a deep breath and then look back at the rest of the table, he said calmly, "You all are correct. Perhaps I overreacted to the situation. I apologize." To the wonderment of all, the fury of Richard McGee had been disarmed by the shiest girl in school.

***

Dr. Diaz stood very somber in the hallway outside of the senior English class. A few teachers lined up behind him. Students stood behind the media, which had been called to report on the dedication of a plaque that had been made in remembrance of Geoffrey Spencer. As more camera lights flashed, Ricardo Diaz ratcheted up his intensity.

"Mr. Spencer showed great dedication to this noble profession and to his students. We should all strive to emulate his example. Your success was his success. He was the greatest of teachers and the greatest of men. We were all fortunate to have known him and worked with him. He will be missed but not forgotten." Dr. Diaz held up the plaque for everyone to see. "Whenever we walk into this room, we will always remember him and the special light he gave us all."

Dr. Diaz choked up and was surrounded by television cameras as the students filed into the classroom. Richard learned over to Thomas and commented quietly, "Why do the baby boomers always have to give themselves awards and plaques for how great they are? Who are they trying to convince? Themselves or everyone else? Spencer was a good teacher and a nice guy, but this is a bit much, isn't it?"

After the reporters had exhausted all their questions and the photographers had taken all their photos, Dr. Diaz entered the room and clasped his hands. "Now, ladies and gentlemen, we must continue on. It's what Mr. Spencer would have wanted. With that in mind I would like to introduce your new English teacher. His name is Mr. Robert St. Pierre. I am certain that you will extend him every courtesy."

Mr. Robert St. Pierre entered the room with élan and flair. He was dressed in a tan corduroy sport coat, chocolate corduroy pants, a yellow turtleneck, and brown suede boots. The scarf around his neck added, he felt, the perfect accent. As Dr. Diaz left the room and closed the door behind him, Mr. Robert St. Pierre shook the dishwater blond hair out of his eyes, put his hands up to his ample chin, took in a deep breath, and gazed out the window. He appeared deep in thought. He exhaled and paused, stared at the ground, then began rubbing his hands in front of his mouth. He muttered under his breath, "Where to begin, where to begin?" Finally, looking up and over the heads of the students, he bellowed out, "All right, children. Seeing as how I am used to teaching at the university level, and this clearly is not that, you may address me as Instructor or as Mr. Robert St. Pierre. You will participate in class. You will answer logically, and you will refrain from any rustic Midwestern fundamentalist rubbish. I do not expect you to achieve my level of logic— or even that of a college freshman-but you will try. I have a PhD in gender studies with an emphasis in anthropology. My thesis was a comparative analysis of Simone de Beauvoir's understanding that one is not born a woman but becomes one and the totemic structure of Aboriginal society and its kinship system. Mmm, fascinating." He paused to recollect and admire his own work. "I have been published," he said with a sigh, "and, as such, I will be very selective in the grading of your papers. I will not accept simplistic, childish banter. For example, using the word 'park' when 'arboretum' is preferred. Is that clear?"

Richard McGee sat straight up in his chair like a lion eyeing up a lamb for slaughter. "Excuse me, Mr. Robert St.

Pierre." Richard had managed to make his name sound like Mr. Robespierre, which was not appreciated by Mr. Robert St. Pierre. "I am confused. There is something I do not understand because I am only a child. Why would you have a preference for the word 'arboretum' in the example given? Isn't that the place where loose women go to kill their babies?"

CHAPTER 11

Eighty degrees in September was common in Chicago but not for six days in a row. Summer was trying to give a final taste of warmth and ease to help carry the memory through until the far-off spring. As autumn induced forgetfulness, winter would soon hammer away with a dark, bone-chilling relentlessness and try to dash any hope for the return of bliss. No matter how ferocious its efforts and how black the night would become, the spring sun would rise in due time to beckon the world back to light and life.

Margaret Clarke stood in the backyard, reveling in the early evening quiet and deciding how to prepare her garden for the next year: what to leave in, what to cut back, what to take out, what to cover in compost or mulch, what to plant in the spring. The carrots and green beans did well this year, but it was time to rotate their position in the bed. Maybe some potatoes would be better if the pH in the soil was right. As she was about to head into the kitchen, the front doorbell rang. Quickly rinsing her hands, she came up to the door, feeling slightly concerned about the small mess her husband and daughter had made before they went out for a walk. A coloring book, crayons, and the front section of the newspaper were enough for Margaret to forget about what Thomas had mentioned a few days earlier. She opened the door, and her eyes welled up.

"Hello, Mrs. Clarke," Marie Martin said nervously.

Overcome, Margaret's hand slowly came up to her mouth. She gently took Marie's hands, kissed her on the forehead, then embraced her as if Marie had been her own child, missing for past three years. What pain and sorrow this young girl had suffered in that time. There was nothing Margaret could do about the past, but for today and into the future, Marie would know without any doubt that this home was her home as well and that the people here loved her.

Margaret took Marie, who was a few inches taller now, by the arm. She was wearing a modest dress and no makeup, but what a beautiful young lady she had become. The memories flooded back: the countless times Marie had been here as a child playing, the numerous hours of practicing piano, and the private moments when the young girl had confided in Margaret problems and fears she could not tell her own mother. Marie wiped away a small tear as Mrs. Clarke led her inside.

Thomas was in his room when he heard the doorbell, and he came quickly down the stairs. He said "hello" to Marie and was surprised when his mother intercepted him and asked if he would get her gardening hat from the yard. His mother's face was flushed, and Marie had only waved in reply to his greeting. Confused, he went out to retrieve the hat. It only took a minute or so before he returned, but now Marie and his mother were composed, smiling, and catching up on things as they sat in the living room by the 1975 Kimball grand piano.

"Marie, how did your recital go on Friday?" Thomas asked.

"It went well, I think." Marie was being modest, and Mrs. Clarke nodded in approval. Marie asked, "Would you like to hear it?"

"Very much so."

Thomas and his mother sat on the couch as Marie settled in on the familiar piano bench. She took a breath and began softly and deliberately coaxing J. S. Bach out of the wood, ivory, and steel. After a few minutes, she was done.

"That was beautiful, Marie," Margaret said.

"*Schafe Können Sicher Weiden,* right?" Thomas asked, smiling.

"Yes, it was. I don't get to practice as much as I would like, so there were a few bumps. Sorry," Marie replied, knowing it was his favorite piece.

"None that I heard. And this piano is here whenever you would like to play it," Margaret said firmly.

While giving thanks for the generous offer, Marie's composure wavered just a bit, but she quickly looked around and observed that the Clarke home appeared a little different. Thomas offered to show her around so that his mother could clean up her gardening materials and straighten up in the kitchen and dining room.

The house was very similar to what Marie remembered, but there had been some changes: new bushes had been planted in front; the dining room had been repainted, which lightened up the living room as well; and Kathleen now had the bigger first-floor bedroom that her grandparents had slept in. That meant Thomas was upstairs by himself in the same bedroom, while Kathleen's old room was now used for storage. The home itself, though, had the same safe, warm embrace Marie had always been both accustomed and drawn to. The furnishings in the house were modest at best, but they were never what made this place feel like a home to anyone who entered through the front door.

Out of habit, Thomas led Marie up the stairs and showed her Kathleen's old room. Margaret, in the kitchen, smiled at the rumbling sound of footsteps above her. So often in the past, Thomas and his childhood friends would be in those rooms playing games and having fun. Kathleen's old room was especially popular as a place for hiding while playing Hide and Go Seek because it had two closets and because it wasn't in Thomas's room, where the counting of the seeker was happening. That was an echo of a time long past. The next children Margaret would hear playing up there again would likely be her grandchildren.

Walking into his own room, Thomas turned and noticed Marie standing in the hallway, near the door. She had been in this room many times in the past, but today it was different, and Thomas suddenly felt uncomfortable and embarrassed to be with her here. Marie peeked her head into the room and saw familiar pictures and awards hanging up, along with a few new ones. The bookcase overflowed even more so than usual. On the wall next to it was a huge map of the universe as well as a picture of Thomas's grandparents. Both were recent additions.

Thomas called the map and the picture his "humility reminders." The map showed the Milky Way galaxy and the Earth's position in it, about 26,000 light years from the center in the Orion spiral arm. There were 200 to 600 billion stars in the Milky Way alone, and the map then extrapolated out to show an estimate of where this galaxy was in relation to the other galaxies, then to galaxy superclusters, then to other local superclusters, then finally to the observable universe. Marie was impressed by the incomprehensible estimated size of the universe but did not see how humility factored into it. Thomas explained that in relation to all of it, he was nothing more than a tiny little speck of dust.

"The picture of my grandparents is a reminder of death. Part of self-knowledge is realizing one's mortality. My grandparents were the most loving people I have ever known, but they died . . . like we all will. I was fortunate to have had the example that they set for me." Marie remembered how hard it had been at the beginning of eighth grade when both of Thomas's grandparents died about the same time that her grandmother passed away. Thomas paused before continuing, "Whenever I am tempted to think that I am something I am not, these things bring me back to reality, to the truth. Humility is nothing more than accepting the truth." He could say things like that in conversation only to Marie. "Come on, let's head downstairs."

Margaret Clarke had her kitchen in order once again and was pouring glasses of lemonade as Thomas and Marie came and sat at the table. Mrs. Clarke asked about Mrs. Martin, and Marie gave a polite but slightly cryptic answer. The three began to talk casually and comfortably about fond memories and what had been missed over the past few years.

Thomas remembered when he and Marie were seven years old and had gotten caught outside in the rain. Marie had stepped on a big worm with her bare feet. He was certain that the echo of her scream could still be heard in the far reaches of the stratosphere. Marie countered with the story of a sixth-grade football game when Thomas, the quarterback who was not allowed to play defense, was on the sideline, not paying attention when the opposing team's running back got tackled on the sideline by four St. Titus Cretans. The grown men holding the down markers, Thomas, and two other players all got pushed by the pile of tacklers into a massive, filthy puddle. They all became covered in mud, but somehow the chain from the down markers also got caught in Thomas's pants. When he stood up, the back of his pants completely ripped open right in front of Marie and the other cheerleaders.

The sound of the front door opening disrupted the conversation. John and Kathleen Clarke returned from their walk and were chatting away themselves when

Kathleen turned and looked in the kitchen. Her eyes went wide, and she yelled out joyfully, "Marie!" Sprinting into the kitchen and placing Marie in a bear hug, which was returned in kind, Kathleen said with a beaming smile, "Marie, I missed you so much. I am so happy you are here."

John added warmly, "That is pretty much how we all feel, Marie."

Marie finally lost her composure, and tears streamed uncontrollably down her red cheeks. "Thank you," was all she could muster in reply. Margaret gave her some tissues, and Kathleen told her everything would be all right. Thomas wanted to kick himself for not offering her an invitation to come over earlier.

Marie collected herself, and Kathleen sat in the adjoining chair, looking at her intently before saying emphatically, "You are beautiful. I hope I look as beautiful as you do when I am in high school." Marie blushed. Kathleen asked Thomas, "Don't you think she looks beautiful, too?" He agreed but did not elaborate on how he was beginning to see the many levels of her beauty.

John Clarke awkwardly broke in and mentioned that he had to work the past Friday. He asked Thomas about his first football game. The West Ridge Raccoons had lost six to nothing, but the team was decent, especially the defense. They would not give up a lot of points, but scoring points would be a problem. The coach called running plays exclusively. The Daniel Boone Pioneers figured that out early, loading up the defensive line with nine defenders. The West Ridge running back, Rex Burger, wasn't a bad athlete, but he played very softly, avoiding contact. There was a chance to tie the game late in the fourth quarter after a Pioneer fumble at their own 20 yard line. The Boone safeties and cornerbacks had pinched in and were ignoring the West Ridge receivers. Thomas tried to suggest a pass, but that idea was dismissed. Another running play was called, and Rex was tackled for a big loss as the clock ran out.

"But at least I kept my pants on for the whole game, though," Thomas commented. John didn't know what that was supposed to mean, but Margaret and Marie laughed.

Kathleen went on questioning, "Do you remember when you used to brush and braid my hair? You could make it look so fancy." Marie nodded in the affirmative. "Maybe you can do it again sometime? My mom fixes my hair now, and it looks nice, but it's not like you used to do. I don't think she would mind if you did it once in a while."

"I would not mind one bit," Margaret added. Marie said she would love to when she had time.

Kathleen was elated but then followed up with a very hard question for Marie, "How come you have not come over here in such a long time? Was it because of what happened to your dad? That was very sad."

John spoke up again quickly. Margaret had to get back to her garden, and Kathleen and he would have to be going now if they wanted to make the next showing of *Kung Fu Panda* at the New 400 Movie Theater. Thomas and Marie were invited to come along, but they declined. John again told Marie how good it was to see her and that he hoped to see her at the Clarke home more often. Kathleen said good-bye with a bear hug and a kiss on the cheek. As Thomas went to help his father and sister get ready to leave, Margaret gave Marie a hug, whispered something in her ear, then returned to the backyard. Marie nodded with a grin, and the three departed.

Thomas came back into the kitchen and took out the pitcher of lemonade to refill their glasses. As he was closing the refrigerator door, he gently asked Marie how she and her mother have been doing, really. Marie thought back to the start of eighth grade at St. Titus—how the school year started out with plans for cheerleading, homecoming dances, a Christmas recital, and graduation parties. After that, she would move on with the rest of her classmates as freshmen at St. Titus High School. That was only four years ago. It suddenly seemed to her now like such a short time, but how things can change in a short time.

Only three months after her grandmother died, her father, James Martin, went out with some of his friends after work, had some drinks, and then decided to drive home. He veered into oncoming traffic, and the head-on collision killed him and the driver of the other car. Marie and her mother were devastated.

"It was difficult for both of us, Thomas," Marie replied with a sigh. "It was especially tough for my mother. The time right after the accident was very hard, but everyone in the parish, especially you and your family, helped us through it. I never thanked you for that. Still, I was angry and confused, and I prayed for the pain to end. It didn't. When we graduated and my mom decided to move, I did not know what I would do. My grandmother, my father, and my friends were all gone. We only moved a mile and a half away, but it felt like a thousand miles. I was alone and continued to pray without any answer. None of it made any sense at all until I read *The Interior Castle,* which you had given to me the summer before. Only then did I come to understand the great gift of suffering."

"A stumbling block and an absurdity for many," Thomas answered, having read St. Teresa of Avila in seventh grade.

"Yes, it is. I love my family, yet my soul has so little love in it compared to the soul of Christ. He willingly suffered for my redemption, to reunite me with God, and he saw the great satisfaction his suffering gave. His perfect love of the Father was shown by his complete obedience to the Father. Then, like St. Teresa, when I looked at a crucifix, it became very clear that there was nothing truly worthy of this great God that I could offer to him or give up for his sake. What greater gift could God give me than a life which was an imitation of that lived by his own beloved Son? This was a greater gift than the one I had prayed for. So, I offered up my suffering, and God united my small cross with the great one Jesus suffered, making both into one. You know, for all that I have been given, if God only requires that I should give up my will in return, that is really not so much to ask for when you think about it."

Thomas was amazed. This certainly was not the shy, frail girl he had known four years ago. That life for her ended abruptly when her father died.

Marie continued, speaking very serenely. "In due time, the anger and the pain ceased, and they were replaced by sweet consolations of patience, peace, and joy. I have never done anything to deserve that. Once you have had a small taste of the heavenly and eternal, all things earthly pale in comparison. God had brought a greater good out of evil. That horrible day was allowed to happen, and you and your family were taken away from me for a short time so that—through suffering—I could come to know and love God better. My suffering was not punishment but purification. Now, I am thankful for everything—the joyful and the painful—for everything is a grace."

Thomas was thankful beyond words that such a beautiful creature had been placed in his life. Where there is beauty, there is goodness, truth, life, and love. He was concerned, though, about Marie's mother and inquired once more about her.

"Are you asking if my mother sees suffering as a gift? No, she does not." Marie became very reflective. Anne Martin's faith had very shallow roots, and she did not believe that God listened to any prayers, so she did not bother with them, allowing bitterness and despair to creep into her heart and plant deep roots of their own.

The Martins' house in St. Titus parish became difficult for Anne to afford on her nurse's salary alone, so it was sold after Marie graduated. Luckily, the price they received was enough to pay off the mortgage and all the other debts. When Grandmother Josephine had died a few months earlier, Anne and her brother, Frank, inherited the two-flat apartment in St. Aloysius parish that they had grown up in. Frank had his own family and home nearby, so Anne and Marie moved in. The building needed some work, but there was no mortgage, and the upstairs apartment provided additional income. However, the main reason they moved was because Anne preferred to be depressed and isolated, resenting and rejecting the kindness and help of her friends from St. Titus. She was not concerned with how this move affected her daughter.

"That is another cross for me to bear," Marie said, "and I will bear it willingly for my mother. Because our society is so full of pride and vanity, I believe those who understand the value of suffering and who are able to suffer should do so to the greatest extent possible."

Thomas assured her, "You won't have to do it alone, Marie."

Marie smiled sweetly, taking a drink of lemonade. "I am happy to hear you say that, Thomas, because there is something I have wanted to ask you."

"Anything."

"Do you suppose that we should only offer up our suffering for those we love? Or should we also offer up suffering for those who hate us?"

"Well, love of your enemy is a very unique aspect of our faith, and it is very difficult for most. But why love imperfectly when you could love perfectly?"

"Very true, but how many people do you suppose understand that as well as you do?"

"I don't know. Some probably better, some probably worse."

Thomas looked confused, so she asked him, "How many people today do you suppose understand the true meaning of suffering as well as the metaphysical nature and origin of truth and its relationship to goodness, beauty, and life? How many can articulate the interrelationship of them all, along with happiness and freedom, in a clear manner?"

He was still unsure where Marie was going with this as she continued, "Well, please believe me, I cannot. Most people cannot, but you can. You have been given a rare gift of wisdom, and you must be more willing to speak up when people say ridiculous things that are false."

Thomas acknowledged, "When you speak, you give words life, substance, and meaning. It is wise to be cautious and practice temperance when speaking only to say that which is good and true. A wise individual does not repeat foolish drivel but allows it to die away. If you speak it again, you give it life it does not deserve." He paused and then asked, "Are you talking about when Richard gets worked up and goes on one of his tangents? Those are meaningless. Usually it is best to just let him wind down on his own because pride blocks the spirit of wisdom and the spirit of truth. No matter what you say to someone whose heart is filled with prideful nonsense, it won't register. They just won't listen."

"What you just explained is exactly what I am talking about. People understand when you say it, but they have trouble on their own. I am not just referring to Richard but to every circumstance. There are a lot of false statements made by those who profess expertise of some kind, and if enough people repeat those false statements long enough, the false statements begin to be widely accepted as true. I did not understand how much horrible misery ignorance of the truth can cause until I saw my mother try to handle the tragedy of my father's death on her own. She is in this darkness, and it draws her in more and more. Every day it breaks my heart, and there are countless multitudes out there in the same condition because too many people accept falsehood for truth."

Thomas felt uncomfortable with what Marie suggested. It went against his quiet and reticent nature. "I see what you are saying, but no one likes a know-it-all. I detest condescending people who claim that your life would be so much better if you only were as perfect as they claimed to be. Isn't living a quiet life of suffering better?"

"Certainly, but it is incorrect to assume that people today have a true understanding of suffering and many other higher things. I am not asking you to preach at anyone, and I know full well there are people who you cannot reason with. But how can you expect anyone to live a life of humble virtue when humility and virtue have been ridiculed, demeaned, and dismissed as something worthless? How can a parent pass on any virtue to a child if the parent never acquired virtue in the first place?"

"You cannot give what you do not possess, whether it is virtue, truth, or a million dollars," Thomas conceded.

Marie pressed on, "So, shall we stand by and let the world stumble into further darkness and misery, or should we make every effort to humbly speak and live the truth in every way possible? I ask you to simply use the gifts you have been given."

She scored a point there. Those who are most able to lead must lead, or else disorder would follow. Order is preferable to disorder in every instance. But what she was asking of him would be a tremendous headache, and he was still unsure, of himself more than anything.

"Marie, honestly, I feel completely unsuited for what you ask. No one would listen to me, although Athanasius against the world does comes to mind also."

"Do you suppose that I would let you do this alone?"

Thomas laughed, and Marie could sense his opposition wavering. She asked him why he gave the speech that he did for admittance to the AP/Honors Club.

"Happiness, peace, and freedom come from the perfection of virtue. I believe that is the truth. Truth is all that matters," he replied. "Even though my ability to reason is imperfect, and my understanding of truth is also imperfect, a wise man follows one path of learning and understanding truth until he comes across a better, higher path of learning and understanding truth. Then he leaves behind the lesser things and goes on to higher things. There is no better or higher teaching on achieving happiness and peace than the perfection of virtue. If there is one, I will be happy to hear it."

"People do want to know truth. In your speech, so many things were presented that the audience there had never heard before and would never have imagined on their own. You spoke in a way that was not only clear and logical but also sincere. You believed what you were saying. For many days after, people came up to Richard and me and peppered us with a million questions about your speech, but our answers were inadequate. They were afraid to approach you because they thought you would make them look foolish for asking. That speaks volumes about their character. William and Susan were the only ones with courage to approach you directly."

"Well, you never begin to truly learn anything until you accept your own ignorance. Of all there is to know in the universe, what's in my little pea brain accounts as nothing."

"Those reminders in your room upstairs are working. You know, Richard was almost as happy as I was to find out you were coming to West Ridge Prep. For three years, he tried to make the same points you did in your speech, but he would get all worked up and frustrated, lecturing and berating people. When you spoke, people listened. What they do with it afterward, of course, is up to them."

Pondering Marie's words carefully, Thomas's mind was now fully engaged, running at a blistering pace. Plato taught that it is best to be especially careful when you debate a point or chastise someone, not to let emotions overcome you and your speech. A loose tongue equals a weak, foolish mind. According to Petrarch, to think that an old established lie is the truth and to think that a newly discovered truth is a lie is like saying truth is a daughter of time. All of this is the height of stupidity.

Most importantly, he could not allow himself to fall into the modern error of Sameness, or the idea that "I am as good as you," as C. S. Lewis would describe it. We may all be equal under the law, but each individual is distinct from the next, each with different talents and in differing amounts. We are not all the same. As Lewis's character Screwtape would be elated to see, the idea of Sameness would lead to a nation without great men and women. Instead, they become subliterate, undisciplined, morally weak, pridefully self-assured from a flattery based on ignorance, and soft from an easy life. Thomas understood the magnitude of what Marie was asking, and it showed plainly on his face. Humility would be the key, but he admitted freely that he had a long way to go in perfecting virtue.

She took his hand in hers. "Allow me to paraphrase St. Teresa. God could perfect a soul in virtue in an instant. How much better is it when we come to perfect virtue by willingly suffering trial for love of God and love of neighbor, even those neighbors who hate us? God gives individuals of great learning a certain instinct to give light to the world. He won't look at the magnitude of anything they do, only at the love with which they do it. After all the damage that worldly pride has inflicted, shouldn't we at least do what we can, no matter how small or insignificant, with the gifts we have been given? We can count on God's grace to fill in what is missing."

Again, he was amazed at Marie's words and demeanor. The innocence of childhood had been ripped away from her against her will, and she had been given a hard life of suffering. Nevertheless, she sat before him today as the living embodiment of humble faith, hope, and charity, heroically and happily accepting her difficulties and adulthood at a very young age. Thomas now believed that his reserved nature was the nature of his childhood. Marie was politely asking him to leave it behind, endure some discomfort, and suffer a few fools. He was not a child anymore, and he had no desire to remain one. This was a call to arms, and he was being urged to manfully step into the breach without fear or trepidation. Underneath the soft, delicate exterior beauty of Marie Martin beat the heart of a warrior, and she had roused the heart of Thomas Clarke into battle.

CHAPTER 12

The moon sat low in a cloudless sky, with every lunar valley and crater clearly detailed. Its mass and radiant glow naturally drew the eye toward it and away from the surrounding blanket of stars. It had rained earlier in the day, and the autumn night was now cool and crisp, but the smell of blood and sweat hung thick in the air. Two groups of young men had armed themselves and squared off to defend their own territory and to launch brief attacks on their opponent. Victory or defeat would be determined by the strategic and tactical application of violence.

Josh Loder, standing over the crumpled heap of a running back from Phillip Armour High, arched his back and let loose a howl that filled the entire stadium. The condensation of his exhaled breath mushroomed into the night and dissipated as the West Ridge Raccoons' defensive lineman then bent over and screamed into the face of the dazed player, who had just fumbled. The energy in the stadium intensified as West Ridge, trailing six to two, recovered the loose ball on the Armour 35 yard line with ninety seconds left to play.

The game had been a grind from the start. The Packers of Phillip Armour High were two-time defending conference champions, though this squad did not have the talent of years past. West Ridge had them in size and speed, but the Packer coaches had their team disciplined and well prepared. Coach Green, on the other hand, stuck with his offensive scheme of one run up the middle, a misdirection play, a sweep, and a punt. The Packer coaches quickly adjusted and filled the defensive line to stop the run. Consequently, the game stalemated early.

In the second quarter, Armour had scored their only touchdown after a long, hard drive that capitalized on some fundamental West Ridge mistakes. Two very talkative Packer offensive linemen, setting up for the extra point, made a few passing comments to Jeff Loder. No one else heard what was said, but the Packers did not get the extra point, and the West Ridge defense had a fire lit under it from that point on. The Packer offense was smothered for the rest of the game, but the West Ridge offense was equally inept. Jeff Loder and his defensive mates became enraged at their head coach. They were playing their hearts out, overcoming the opponent's advantage in leadership with sheer effort and will.

Every series was the same: one Raccoon defensive player after the next would make an outstanding play, only to come off the field to watch their offense try the same three handoffs and then punt. The offensive players' effort was there; that of the head coach was not. Early in the fourth quarter, when Armour was pinned inside their own 10 yard line, the Packer coaches told the quarterback to run out of the end zone for a safety. It gave West Ridge two points, but they knew the Raccoon offense could not score any points on its own. Armour could ride the clock out for the rest of the game and win six to two.

This had become a game that not only could be won, it had to be won. West Ridge had a better team, and they were outplaying the opposition. At the end of the fourth quarter, the Raccoons were physically exhausted, but more so, they were tired of losing. Every second that ticked off the clock let the elusive grasp of victory, which was so close at hand, slip through their fingers. Frustration and anger burned away inside them as the Packer offense lined up for one last set of downs. It was then that Jeff Loder mustered up one last burst of energy, fired through a gap, and planted the Packer running back into the ground with a furious tackle. After a mad scramble for the ball, the referees signaled a change in possession. The crowd roared with anticipation, and the defensive coaches had to restrain some of the players coming off the field from getting near the head coach.

A call went out for the offense to take the field. Thomas grabbed his helmet and looked at the clock: one minute and thirty seconds with one time-out. The stadium seats and both sidelines were filled with electricity. Coach Green and the offensive coaches were having a heated argument. Keeping his distance, Thomas asked what the play was. Coach Green put an end to the discussion and replied impassively, "R formation, 32 pop."

Running onto the field, Thomas noticed some of the other coaches walking away in disgust. In the huddle, he called the play, but there was a whistle to temporarily halt the game. Armour needed more time to tend to the injured running back and get him off the field, and then the team grumbling began. "This is a stupid play. We're going to lose again. How could the coach call another straight handoff right up the middle?"

The referee blew the whistle to resume play, and West Ridge came up to the line. Thomas normally would count the defensive backs and call out the defensive formation so that his linemen could make adjustments, but there were no defensive backs. West Ridge had a flanker lined up in the backfield just off the outer hip of the left tackle, the tight end was a foot next to the right tackle, and the other flanker was in the backfield just off of the tight end's hip. Rex was behind Thomas in the middle of an inverted wishbone. Steve Souter was split wide left, fifteen yards out. There was one defender out there in coverage but with eyes solidly in the backfield. The rest of the defense packed around the ball on the line of scrimmage. The play that had been called had no chance of success.

A goal line set was called out, and as the ball was snapped, two blitzing linebackers were in the backfield to meet Rex as he took the handoff. Earlier in the game, Rex would have run away from the defenders or simply fallen down. Now with fatigue setting in, Rex had no energy left for diversion. Vengeful Packers were on him before there was time to react. Payback was dished out, and Rex was hammered for a 4-yard loss. He let out a whimpering cry of anguish.

He staggered to his feet, and the clock kept running until someone on the West Ridge sidelines called a time-out. Thomas ran over to complete chaos. Players were arguing with other players, coaches with other coaches, players with coaches, coaches with fans. There was just over a minute left in regulation, and Coach Green called for the same formation and a sweep to the right. That set off another round of bickering as Thomas ran back to the huddle.

Rex was still groggy and not happy about being hit on the last play. When he stated with a sniveling, high-pitched whine that the line had better block for him this time, Thomas had to push the incensed linemen out to get set before a delay of game penalty was called. He took the snap, opened left, and spun around 180 degrees, pitching the ball to Rex. Rex bobbled it, dropped it, and then chased it out of play before getting crushed again by a swarm of Packer defenders. This time there was loud sobbing, and the defense almost showed some pity for the pathetic nature of it all. The referees threw a flag for the hit out of bounds, and the clock stopped with forty-two seconds to play.

Rex was down and showed no sign of getting up. A trainer put a hand in front of Rex's face and asked how many fingers he saw. The groggy reply was "Uh, Tuesday." Coach Green lifted him up and pushed him back on the field. When Thomas asked for the next play, the coach closed his eyes hard for a second and then told him to just take a knee. Coach Green had had enough of this game, his coaches, the players, and the fans. As his quarterback ran back to the huddle, the coach bent over, threw down his clipboard, and tried to massage his temples to get some relief from his splitting headache. He missed what was happening on the field.

Thomas came in, crouched down, and calmly looked at each player in the huddle. Except for Rex, everyone else was angry and jawing away, not really saying anything in particular, just voicing their frustration as they came to realize that this game was going to be lost.

"Listen to me," Thomas said sharply. The huddle suddenly drew quiet. "We are going to win this game right now."

The fans could see a short animated discussion before the Raccoons broke the huddle and came up to the line in their usual formation. That put big smiles on the faces of the Packer defenders, and they began to taunt West Ridge players on the sidelines and on the field, especially Rex. Thomas came up behind the center and scanned the field; there were no defensive backs to be seen. As he called out the goal line set, the right flanker split out ten yards wide, while the left flanker dropped into the backfield next to Rex.

"What the hell?" was all Coach Green could mutter before he tried to call a time-out. The side referee generously told him he had none left. The Packer linebackers began calling out in a panic for their people to shift, and the entire defense was in a momentary state of total confusion. Before the defense could organize or call a time-out, Thomas quick snapped the ball and opened left, hesitated, then spun right to hand off to the backfield flanker, who had opened with a jab step left, then cut back hard right. A few Packers yelled out "counter, counter, counter," and the mass of the defense shifted up toward the line and to the offense's right. Thomas slammed the ball into the flanker's gut and peeled off left as the outnumbered and overwhelmed offensive linemen put up a valiant fight to buy a few seconds of time. The flanker crashed into an immoveable wall and went down in a heap. Packer shouts of victory were short lived as they looked up into the backfield to see the West Ridge quarterback on his toes with the football cocked at his ear, ready to fire.

Steve Souter was racing down the sidelines directly in front of the dejected Phillip Armour coaching staff. Crossing the goal line, a bullet pass hit him in the chest right between the numbers and knocked him to the ground. He got up in a delirium, surrounded by a surge of teammates, coaches, fans, and people he had never seen before, all patting him on the back, yelling, and screaming. The sound was deafening, and he was not sure what exactly had happened, but at that moment—and for the first time in history—Steve and the West Ridge Raccoons were winners.

CHAPTER 13

"Hello, Ms. Wilson. I am here to see Dr. Diaz," Thomas said politely but in what had become an all-too-familiar manner. He sat down in his usual chair and waited for the yelling in the other room to finish. When everything had quieted down, the secretary gave it a few moments, then let the principal know who was waiting for him. Thomas walked into the freshly repainted office and took a seat in the big leather chair. No matter how routine these meeting were becoming, the view of the city out the window was always spectacular.

"Mr. Clarke, so good to see you again. Let me congratulate you on the big win last Friday." It had been five days, but the last-second football victory was still the talk of the school. Principal Diaz didn't really care about the game, except it allowed him to puff out his chest and scoff at the principal of Phillip Armour High.

"Thank you, sir. It is good to see you again as well," Thomas replied, noticing that there had been more perspiring than usual after the last phone call.

"Mr. Clarke, I am going to get right to it," Dr. Diaz said very seriously. It unsettled the man a great deal that he could not get any kind of emotional response out of this kid no matter what was said to him. "I have been receiving some disturbing reports lately. Shocking, really. I asked for you to come here today so that you can explain your side of the latest incident."

"Incident? I don't know what incident you are referring to, sir."

"Come now, Mr. Clarke. The incident earlier today in Mr. Robert St. Pierre's English class? I think you know what I am talking about."

"Sir, I am not aware of any incident that happened in class today. It was like every other day."

"Are you saying that you and Mr. McGee did not gang up on Mr. St. Pierre to embarrass him?"

So that's what this is about, Thomas thought to himself. He delicately explained, with very nuanced language, that Richard had been tormenting the man for weeks, apparently with some success, to the point where Mr. St. Pierre became extremely sensitive to anyone questioning anything he said.

A few weeks prior, the instructor had made a statement to the effect that an AP/Honors student could do anything they wanted to do in life if they would only apply themselves. Thomas inquired about the truth of that statement and explained that people cannot make themselves into something they are not. They either have an ability or a talent for something, or they don't. Thomas would never understand mathematics or physics like Pythagoras, Newton, or Einstein. Also, no matter how hard he tried, Thomas would never be a professional quarterback in the NFL.

Mr. St. Pierre tried to stifle this talk, but to his chagrin, William chimed in and agreed with Thomas. The other students also openly agreed with Thomas. Even Scott Weber, usually a steadfast supporter of Mr. St. Pierre, admitted that he could never be a surgeon because he couldn't stand the sight of blood. Naturally, Richard decided to ratchet things up some by innocently questioning "Mr. Robespierre" as to why so many adults deliberately lie to and deceive children by telling them such foolish baby boomer propaganda.

Earlier today, Thomas continued, Mr. St. Pierre had made another statement on a trivial subject that Richard took exception to. Richard stated that it was not true. Mr. St. Pierre challenged him to prove it. Richard countered that one cannot prove a negative. "What does that mean exactly?" the teacher had quickly retorted. "People say that all the time, but I don't believe they really know what they are talking about." Richard stumbled badly trying to explain it himself before desperately looking over to Thomas for help.

Thomas initially did not do much better when he put it forth that either something is, or it is not. It cannot be both. Something cannot be and not be at the same time. Something that is can be proven because it is. Something that is not cannot be proven because it is not. If something is not, it has no existence. Strictly speaking, something that is is whole and complete. Something that is not is deficient.

Thomas could see from the glazed look in the eyes of Mr. St. Pierre that the scholastic approach was not going to work, so Thomas asked to go up to the board to clarify his statements. The nature of truth and being are in alliance; they are the same. Something is true if it is whole and complete, deficient in nothing, lacking in nothing. Because there is no deficiency, truth is perfect. Because there is no deficiency and because it is perfect, truth will never change from that state of perfection. It is immutable. Because it is perfect and will never change from that state of perfection, it is eternal. The nature of truth and existence, along with beauty and goodness, is that they are whole and complete, without deficiency and not lacking in any way. They are unchanging, perfect, and eternal. Something is true when it is in accord with the nature of truth itself.

Thomas placed a piece of paper on Dr. Diaz's desk and drew a circle on it in the same way that he drew one on the board in class to show visually how the true circle had no beginning and no end. It was eternal. The line would continue to go around and around perfectly, without change. He then erased a section of the circle and stated that it could no longer truly be called a circle because it was now deficient in what a circle requires to be a circle. People may say it is kind of like a circle or that it is pretty much like a circle, but strictly speaking, it is not a circle. Thomas continued by explaining that while he can show there is a deficiency in this curved line that prevents it from being called a true circle, he cannot prove the existence of the nothingness that comprises that deficiency.

Then, Mr. St. Pierre, in a fit of misology, declared that he would decide for himself what was true and what was not, and Thomas countered that that was illogical and impossible. One plus one cannot equal three simply because a person desires it. One plus one must equal two. That has been true from the beginning of time, it is true this very instant, and will always be true into the future; that is unchanging, perfect, and eternal. The truth of the statement that one plus one equals two is not dependent on anyone agreeing with it, accepting it, or even understanding it. One plus one cannot equal three. One plus one will always equal two and can never be anything other than that.

After this thorough explanation, Thomas concluded by asking, "Is that what you mean by the incident, sir? The entire discussion was routine for the classroom."

Ricardo Diaz did not like to concentrate on any one thing for very long and had lost track of what was being said. The other students he had already talked with were in agreement that the discussion was civil and respectful, and they all repeated that they had been compelled by the instructor from the first day to participate in class.

When Dr. Diaz mentioned to Thomas that Mr. St. Pierre had accused him—the most unassuming of students—and Richard of being disruptive in class and having an elitist attitude, Thomas's raised eyebrow would be the most severe emotional reaction the principal would ever have the pleasure to see from him. It was one teacher's word against that of a classroom of top students, and actually, this teacher was only temporary.

During the phone call before this meeting with Thomas, the principal had received information that his main opponent for the superintendent's position was about to score major points in his favor and bolster his image with some very positive press about an afterschool antiviolence program at Dunning High. The local media was going to give wide coverage of all the influential black ministers and various politicians lined up with the mayor to support the new program. Unfortunately, in the mind of Ricardo Diaz, West Ridge Prep was in a much more peaceful neighborhood, so he could not craft a similar program in response. That would have to wait until later; right now the primary goal was to keep any negative press from the public.

Already perspiring profusely and feeling agitated from contemplating the situation, the phone rang and interrupted his train of thought. The principal scolded his secretary angrily, "Charlene, I thought I made myself clear. I—" Quickly hanging up the phone, his face went flush. It was obvious that the ambitious mind of Dr. Diaz was in a frenzy, barely restraining total panic. The collar of this shirt was soaking wet. Thomas was hurried out of the room without the usual niceties, and an emergency meeting was called for all available school staff.

Walking down the hallway toward the cafeteria, there was no indication of anything that could have caused such terror and stress in the principal's office. The only thing that did seem unusual to Thomas was the continual fascination everyone had with last Friday's football game.

Donald Spears came up and continually repeated with emphasis how "schimply fantshtic" and "outschtanding" the game had been. But the events he described were completely different from the game Thomas had participated in. After shaking hands with a group of overly enthusiastic sophomores, Thomas found an inquisitive Richard McGee at their usual lunch table.

"Hey, stud. I hope you are charging your fans a lot of money for all those autographs and pictures."

"That's the thing, Rich. When I looked up in the stands during the game, I saw you, Marie, my parents, and my sister. I was surprised you actually stayed to the end. Thanks for that."

"To be honest, it was touch and go for a while. But I had not seen your family in a few years, and it was nice to talk with them. We all ended up having a great time. Your mom is the kindest person who ever lived, and Kathleen is like her little twin. You dad is a really good guy. He's funny, too. So, what happened to you?" Richard smirked.

"Anyway, by my reckoning, the five of you comprised about 10 percent of the total crowd. All these people who have congratulated me for winning and for making spectacular plays during the game weren't even there. Based on all the feedback, it would seem that the West Ridge stadium had at least ten thousand people in it. I appreciate it when someone comes up and says a kind word, but this is too much. Public praise is just a shifting breath of wind. It has no substance. I don't pay any attention to it."

"It is amazing what one little win will do for people accustomed to losing. It even made you popular."

"We won that game as a team," Thomas replied in the simple, calm, matter-of-fact manner that many people, including Richard, appreciated and respected but that others found so aggravating and distressing. "I just did what I was supposed to do as best as I was able. Expecting special recognition for that is like asking for a pat on the back simply because you have obeyed the law."

"Please don't let any baby boomer hear you say that. They will soon start giving themselves awards because they made it through a whole day without getting arrested and thrown in jail. Although for some of them, it would be a major feat."

"Well, all fame is fleeting, and this will pass soon enough. But, I'm afraid, not as quickly as I would like."

"That's why you have to strike while the flames are hot, my friend. You could make a fortune off of these pigeons."

"I would rather be known as a good man than a rich man."

"Let me see. So far I have heard that the Armour players were all seven feet tall and had just been paroled from prison; that Coach Green had perfectly executed a brilliant, secret game plan that had pulled out a victory from the jaws of defeat; and that you have signed with an agent, are forgoing college, and will soon declare yourself eligible for the NFL draft. If you think all this is going to die down soon, I am going to have to think up some new stuff and start stirring the pot to keep it going." Richard loved to be a big spoon in situations like this.

Thomas thought back to the mayhem of the game and, at the end, how the offensive linemen had physically threatened Steve Souter when he balked at running a different play from what the coach had called. Public opinion never judges anything right and never calls anything by its true name. Richard seemed intent on mayhem, so Thomas changed the topic of conversation and asked why Dr. Diaz was so upset.

"Oh, didn't you see the big protest out in front and all the television cameras?"

Thomas replied in the negative, and Richard went on to describe a group of black ministers, politicians, and parents from the south side neighborhood around Dunning High who had come up to loudly protest what they claimed was the unequal, racist nature of the Chicago public schools. "They say our school not only gets more money than their school, but we also get some kind of secret information here that isn't taught in black schools. That's the reason, they believe, why we do better on the state tests than they do. They are demanding to know why their students are being deprived."

Thomas looked at Richard, studied his face, and asked, "You are being serious, aren't you?"

"I am dead serious. The truth is that Dunning High actually gets more money per student than we do. But our enrollment is much larger here, so the total amount of money we receive is larger also. The other stuff about the secret information is goofy, but some people believe it. I have actually heard it said to my father on many occasions that the only reason there are so many young black men in prison is because those prisoners did not get the secret teaching that white people get. If they only were taught the secret information that, say, Steven Hawking or Robert Goddard received, then all those prisoners would have PhDs in theoretical physics. It's not their fault."

"That's insulting to suggest that anyone's grades come from anything other than natural aptitude and effort. Don't they know we have many minority students here, even in the AP/Honors program?" Thomas asked.

"They don't care. From what I understand, some black people have a big problem when someone else becomes successful, but they especially have a problem when that successful person is black. Supposedly, it can get vicious. Anyway, the protestors got to stick their faces in front of a camera and say what they wanted to say. It is annoying, though. On the one hand, they are demanding the same rights as everyone else and asking to be treated just like everyone else, but on the other hand, they still want special privileges. That's the culture they have chosen."

"You can't blame somebody else for your own shortcomings. What is true for one person is true for all people. Rights and responsibilities are two sides of the same coin, and a successful society demands both. From what you are saying, they are asking to be considered equal citizens but separate. I wonder if the irony of that position is fully understood by the protestors."

"Good luck trying to explain that, but I think that protest is the reason Rick Diaz is running around like a crazy man right now trying to prevent the teachers and staff members from making any embarrassing comments to the press. This whole thing has the smell of politics."

That would certainly explain the hysterics, Thomas reasoned. Thomas was about to get back to his ham on rye when he noticed they were ten minutes into the lunch break. "Where is Marie?"

"She had some music tutoring thing to take care of," Richard replied with a widening grin. "That reminds me, Johnny Football Hero. Someone has been asking me about you; she wanted to know if you had a girlfriend. I said no. Was I correct?"

Thomas gave a look clearly indicating he was not interested in Richard's toying and was not going to delve into personal matters.

"I am just letting you know, Stud Boy." Richard scanned the room. "As a matter of fact, she is sitting right over there." Richard was not going to let it go, so Thomas indulged his folly and turned around. "All right, look at the last table, all the way by the wall. Do you see the girl with blonde hair?" Sitting there was a tall, tanned, stunningly beautiful girl with flowing blonde hair. She was chewing gum and texting on a phone. Thomas nodded in the affirmative when asked if he could see her clearly. Then Richard stated dismissively, "Well, it's not her. Forget about her. You are nothing and nobody to that girl. She doesn't even know you exist."

Thomas had to laugh. He had walked right into that one. "No, that's funny. It really is."

"Anyway, look to the left of the blonde," Richard commanded with a smile. "See the girl six seats down, at the end of the table, dressed like a Bulgarian prostitute? That's the one who was asking about you."

Thomas recoiled when he gazed upon a heavyset girl dressed in a very dark and sloppy manner, but also in a very revealing and inappropriate manner. Her wild, brownish-red hair had streaks of purple and was full of beads and ribbons. There were piercings and hoops of metal scattered about her face and ears, and the varied collection of beads and necklaces around her neck partially covered some kind of patterned tattoo. Her fingers and arms were filled with rings and bracelets.

"Isn't that Monique Sims, Rex's girlfriend?' Thomas asked.

"Well, girlfriend is probably too strong a word. That implies some kind of an emotional attachment. If you meant to ask if she is the inanimate object that Rex consumes alcohol and drugs with and then with which he satisfies his carnal desires, then yes. So, strictly speaking, she is unattached as well. Beastly but unattached. Shall I make the introductions?"

Thomas let Richard have his fun with him, but Thomas did not like his disparaging statements about this girl, no matter how unladylike she appeared.

"Introductions will not be required, thank you. But she is still someone's daughter. You could be a little more respectful with your comments."

"Are you kidding me? Look at this Sasquatch walking up to Monique right now. That's her odious partner in crime Desiree Dubois." She was a tall and ample girl with a huge mane of frizzy hair, and she dressed in a similar way to Monique. Desiree came to Monique's table carrying a tray of food.

"Rich, that's too harsh."

Richard considered Thomas's words for a second and replied, "You're right. My previous statement was false. A Sasquatch is just a brute animal. A Wookie can at least gesture and grunt to communicate. Desiree can certainly do that. So, truth be told, she is closer to a Wookie than a Sasquatch. I stand corrected, sir."

Thomas was about to reply when Desiree stumbled, spilling the contents of her tray all over the floor. She let out a loud, extremely offensive expletive. It was heard by the entire cafeteria. Monique then joined her friend in high-volume, giggle-snort laughter and a stream of foul language that would make a seasoned sailor blush. The blonde at the other end of the table hurried away in disgust.

"Yeah, each of them is somebody's precious little angel all right. What kind of home do you think they grow up in?" Richard shuddered. "Those two toads are about as feminine as Mike Ditka is waking up with a hangover. They're just two pigs from the south side." Richard was beaming. His reputation for insulting others was unchallenged.

"Proud of yourself, are you?"

"Just calling it like it is, pal."

"Tell me, should we value ourselves based on the weaknesses and feebleness of others, or should we value ourselves based on the merit of our own actions?"

Richard let out a long, slow breath and stared up at the ceiling. He admitted, "I hate when you do that."

Thomas continued, masking a slight smile, "Pride that disparages others is worse than that which overestimates itself. If we could only point to a single day well lived. Just as you notice the actions of others, be assured that others take notice of your actions as well. Bother about worth, not about glory. Lack neither example nor reproof. One should preserve one's good name to free one's friends from the shame of having to tell lies about them."

"Enough, enough, enough. How do you remember all that stuff, anyway?" Richard conceded defeat and acknowledged he was wrong to say what he did. Richard disliked the admonitions that Thomas gave him because they would clearly state what Richard always thought to himself after speaking certain unkind words. He was not mean-spirited by nature; rather, he had a weakness in self-control. Too often, things would come out of his mouth that were immediately regrettable and made him feel like an intemperate, foolish child. Richard had given plenty of opportunities for being reproached in his young life, but Thomas was always mild, often humorous, and carefully selective in admonishing his friend.

The Collected Works of Plato had made an impression on Richard recently, provoking him to think about things he had never really considered before. The book had been consuming most of his free time lately, and Richard thanked Thomas for recommending it to him. He also thanked him for his help in class with Mr. St. Pierre.

"No need for thanks," Thomas calmly replied with an easy smile. "You know, Petrarch wrote about how helpful it was to read *Peace of Mind* by Seneca, but as soon as he put the book down, he—like most of us—forgot all the helpful things he had just read. I believe the old saying that the eyes are the window to the soul. The question then becomes, with what should you fill your soul? Most people get a full dose of vulgarity and foolish nonsense just living their life and interacting with other people, but then they go home and fill themselves with even more vulgarity and foolish nonsense in the form of trashy books, magazines, television shows, movies, music, and Internet sites."

"Those things aren't all bad," Richard protested.

"They are not evil by nature, but they are used in a disordered and improper manner. It would be false to claim that those media outlets are utilized primarily for what is good, true, and beautiful."

"I agree with that," Richard replied. Neither he nor Thomas nor Marie spent much time with popular culture.

Thomas continued, "Petrarch's mind at the time was distracted by too many things, thus nothing useful or fruitful could take root. The same is true today. People have become accustomed to possessing numerous contradictory—even idiotic—ideas and holding them all to be equal and worthy of acceptance. I think we ought to fill our soul only with what is true, good, and beautiful, and toss aside the rest. Don't let the beautiful be drowned out by filth."

"What could you possibly propose to replace the wisdom and beauty found on eight million cable and satellite channels?" Richard mustered up his best sarcasm for that question.

"I think you can watch television, go to the movies, listen to music, and use the Internet if you are able. Unless your soul is properly ordered, though, it is far too easy to become overwhelmed by the garbage. So, for most people, it is best to avoid it all completely. Whatever you do, do it well."

"I don't waste my time with most of that hillbilly trash as it is," Richard said repulsively. "You know, when our parents were kids, there were—at most—five or six television stations, and TV was referred to then as the 'idiot box.' Now there are unlimited channels, and all of a sudden it's an invaluable means of communication that no one can do without. We got rid of cable a few years ago, and I don't miss it at all. Most of the shows were just so boring, stupid, and bad at the most basic level, and that's apart from the way they would bombard you with their progressive Hollywood view of the world. Yech! My dad used to have cable for all the news channels, but now he has a couple of lackeys who watch that stuff for him. Good riddance." Richard held his nose with one hand and gave a dismissive wave with the other. "When I go to a movie, I just want to be entertained for a few hours. That's

CHAPTER 13

it. Have some kind of a plot, a little action, a little drama, a little comedy. Not too much, though. I don't need to see entrails being ripped out and brains splattering all over the place. I don't want to see some bimbo disgrace herself in the name of 'art.' I feel too bad for her parents when I see that. And I really don't need to see a supposedly adult male with Peter Pan syndrome acting like a foul-mouthed, irresponsible teenager. I see enough of that in real life. Just keep it simple, please. There hasn't been any decent music made post-1965, and I personally think the Internet is just a megaphone for the ignorant."

Thomas hesitated but then began, "Well, for you then, if you don't mind my saying. . . . "

"Please do."

"Once you get your basic level of understanding from Plato and the Greeks, which is impressive, then you can quickly move on through the Romans to the really useful writings: Holy Scripture, Augustine, the Early Church Fathers, Thomas Aquinas, *The Imitation of Christ,* among others. They fill in where the Greeks and the Romans come up short to give the fullness of Truth. There are, of course, many other worthwhile fields of study: history, languages, mathematics, the natural sciences, literature, poetry, art, music." As he listened to Thomas speak, Richard could only think of Plato's description of the truly educated man who is able to recognize truth in all areas of study. Thomas continued, "All these things are helpful. The best ones, though, will not only give you an understanding of virtue and truth but also of honor and chivalry, or 'proper deportment,' as Marie would say. We each must tear out our vices and plant deep roots of virtue to enjoy peace, happiness, and freedom. If you don't have any bad things getting in the way, the good things will tend to stick with you."

"That sounds like a lot. It could take years to get through it all."

"If you believe what Abbe Faria told Edmond Dantes in the Chateau d'If prison, for a man committed to the task and with the aptitude to learn, it should not take more than two years. Although, they did have a lot of free time on their hands. The point is, some people can do it, and some people can't. I personally believe, though, that one should learn as much and for as long as one is able to learn. It also helps to take notes."

Richard responded, with some pride, that Plato also wrote about the true philosopher being willing to commit his entire life to understanding truth. Thomas agreed and finished his thought, "You and I can know Truth in a way Plato could never imagine. But once Truth is known, you have to act on it. What is the point of amassing all this knowledge if you don't put it to some practical use? There must be a correlation between thought and action. If there is, you will eventually achieve victory over yourself and your weaknesses. As it says in one of my favorite lines from *The Imitation of Christ*, 'the man who has so conquered himself that his flesh is now subject to reason, and his reason is obedient to God in all things, that man is master of himself and lord of the world.'"

Richard McGee was near the top of his class in one of the best academic high schools in the country. He could confidently hold his own and match wits with men twice his age, but he could not escape the fact that Thomas Clarke was his better in intelligence, in manners, and in charity. Thomas was also a good friend. Thomas would admonish Richard to make him a better man, never to denigrate him. Recently, though, Thomas had begun to speak with an impressive, mature confidence and authority, and Richard had become tired of his own embarrassing, childish antics in comparison. It would definitely be a struggle, but he vowed to overcome himself and to improve in all areas, especially as a friend.

"Well," Richard said after contemplating all that had been said, "I think having some kind of hobby certainly doesn't hurt either. You can't always read and study, and you should do something productive with your free time besides texting, watching television, surfing the Internet, and stuffing your face with food and drink. Those things are not hobbies."

"I agree with that. Idle hands are the devil's playground, but gleefully wreaking havoc is not a productive hobby either, you know."

"Well, that may be, but no matter what you say, I am still going to rip on the Bears. They stink." State Representative Charles McGee had been a longtime season ticket holder, recently upgrading to a skybox, which his son believed gave the entire McGee family a kind of duty to hold the Chicago Bears to a certain level of excellence. "Orton or Grossman? Who cares? Throw Brad Maynard out there as quarterback. It doesn't matter. The Bears are just plain bad. And don't get me started on celebrities. Actors, actresses, and models are all fair game."

Thomas smiled, shook his head, and went back to his ham on rye.

CHAPTER 14

It was incredible how slowly the second hand of the clock seemed to move when you paid close attention to it. It ticks away, steady and smooth, around and around, over and over again. Unless it is unplugged or runs out of batteries, it just keeps going.

John Clarke sat at his office desk in silent contemplation, staring up at the clock on the wall. It was a $10 special from Target with an inch-wide silver border surrounding the plain white face and the black numbers and arms. He had bought it a few years ago and never really paid much attention to it, except when he wanted to know the time. With a small and simple mechanism and one AA battery in the back, still the original, the clock had worked perfectly ever since. *Amazing*, he thought.

His work desk was about ten feet away from the wall, and just the faintest sound could be heard from the clip of the second hand moving from one second mark to the next. Off in the back of the print shop was the low, indistinct murmuring of the news on an AM radio station. George could be heard shuffling around, sweeping up for the fourth time today. It was only 11:45 on this brisk Thursday October morning, and there was no work to be done at Clarke Printing. A small order was waiting to be delivered on Friday for Illinois High School Association football, but there was nothing for the rest of the week nor into the near future. The periodic rumbling of a passing train across the street was ignored, and the deafening silence quickly returned.

John allowed himself to drift off with the clock because it took his mind off the bad news that appeared to be everywhere: in newspapers, on TV, on the radio, on the Internet. It was all too difficult to look at. People were not just talking about economic recession anymore; they were now discussing an actual depression. The clock was more peaceful and serene, and he had promised his wife that he would stay away from the media prophets of doom.

He really did not need them to put him in a sour mood. For that, all he had to do was walk out on his floor and see $75,000 worth of new machinery, computers, and software sitting idle. A year and a half earlier, when everything was going well and money was flowing in, it seemed an opportune time to undertake much-needed upgrades and to expand. He had to get a loan of $50,000, which he took out against the previously debt-free building. But with nothing coming in now, that $50,000 loan was burning up a large part of his rapidly depleting savings. At least his house had been paid off many years ago. The fact that he was not swimming in mortgage debt put him in a much better position than most, and it was the only thing keeping him going at this point.

The few orders that trickled in here and there kept them afloat for now, but that would not last long term. Thank God his wife was so resourceful. He reminded himself for the millionth time how lucky he was to have her.

He gazed over at the small picture of his family on his desk, and it instantly lifted his spirits. At the same time, it caused some distress. It was his responsibility to provide for them, and he could see a time coming in the near future when he would not be able to do that anymore—not here anyway. Since Thomas had received his ACT scores, every major university in the country had swamped their house with letters begging Thomas to apply. A few came from overseas as well. But when John had seen the tuition costs, even after generous financial aid had been granted, the estimated totals were staggering. He could barely afford to send Kathleen to a Catholic grammar school. These university tuitions were in a whole different league. But how could he deny Thomas the opportunity? It could very well break him financially, but he would do whatever it took to get Thomas through school and to provide for the rest of his family. Even as the second hand of the clock seemed to move slower and slower, John Clarke was aging rapidly.

When the front doorbell rang, it gave the hope of some new business. That hope was dashed when John saw the slithery representative of Silver Screen Realty waiting outside.

***

The mild start to November had quickly given way to an unwelcome taste of winter. The golden glow of the remaining fall leaves had been blasted away by strong, gusty winds driving a biting, freezing rain that left the trees and their limbs stark and naked under a gray sky. The ominous strength and size of the storm had a grandeur of its own. It was not beautiful by any means, but it served as a powerful warning that nature was taking this part of the world into colder and darker times.

The rain had stopped midmorning, and despite the dreary day, Thomas and Marie were slowly walking home. The last Friday bell always felt like a weight had been temporarily lifted off of their shoulders and that there would be at least a few hours to relax before Monday morning arrived again. The football season had ended the week before, which freed up a few afternoon hours for the two to enjoy together. Neither wanted to waste one second of that precious time.

The West Ridge Raccoons finished with four wins and four losses, with the last six games being much more enjoyable than the first two. After the historic victory of the second game, which had long since been forgotten, Coach Green received glowing accolades for his leadership and coaching acumen following the initial reaction to the win. As a result, he philosophically shifted his role of head coach. No longer would he run the offense, have anything to do with the defense, or bother with setting up and running practices. In fact, he was completely absent on many occasions. He began to see himself as more of a supervisor of the whole program and pushed all of his previous responsibilities onto the younger and more energetic assistant coaches.

The team responded immediately. The disorganized mess that had been in place was replaced by a structured routine that the players, except for Rex, much preferred. The offense became more balanced, and the role of the single running back was reduced considerably. Now, though, they could move the ball, sustain a drive, and put points on the scoreboard. The defense put up the same game effort as before, but instead of acting like a group of wild berserkers in a melee, their attack was focused and effective. Each player, on both sides of the ball, knew what was expected of him on every play. Even though the young coaches made plenty of mistakes, four wins and four loses was about the best they could have expected with the talent on hand. Thomas was satisfied with the result, and Marie was happy he came out of the season in one piece.

They walked along, simply talking and enjoying each other's company. Thomas and Marie went out of their way to find the most picturesque streets, if they could honestly be described that way. The world always seemed distant and unimportant when they were fortunate enough to share a rare few minutes alone.

"What are you and your mother going to do for Thanksgiving, Marie?"

"We were invited to Uncle Frank's house. His wife is a wonderful cook. I am looking forward to it very much." Marie was putting on a brave face. She had been working part time at her uncle's small music school and store in Evanston for the past few years. After working at the counter and sweeping up, she could practice on the piano for a little while. Frank was a good man, and Marie was very fond of him, his wife, and their three small children. It was her mother that Marie was concerned about.

Anne Martin possessed very little emotional restraint to begin with, and when the economy sputtered, every news report would send her from extreme despair to false elation. Marie would try to keep things calm and reassure her mother that they were going to be all right. Fewer hours of overtime at the St. Aloysius Hospital were not going to put them in debtor's prison. Nothing Marie said or did had any effect. Her mother would become inconsolable. Common sense and reason fell on deaf ears. Sitting at home alone, Anne would let her mind be spun into a frenzied hurricane, conjuring up every possible and impossible situation that could occur to bring ruin on her and her daughter and lamenting over the perfect bliss once enjoyed in a time long past that never actually existed. She would also become convinced that Marie was going to sneak off in the middle of the night, move far away, and leave her all alone. After a few days, the storm would pass. Mrs. Martin would then decide that things were never better and chastise her daughter for worrying about her too much. The emotional roller coaster was very difficult for Marie.

At every holiday since her husband's death, Anne would be mostly pleasant company unless there was alcohol involved. Despite everything that had happened, she occasionally drank too much, and her paper-thin self-restraint vanished, embarrassing herself and Marie in front of their relatives. Uncle Frank and his wife usually kept things under control at their house, but when they came to Anne and Marie for Christmas, anything could happen.

As Marie took Thomas's arm and explained all this, she looked away and seemed uncharacteristically melancholy. Her mother was not the only sadness in her heart. Marie had just finished filling out college entrance applications, and she knew that Thomas had recently done the same. He had applied to many universities scattered across the nation. There was a very real possibility that he could go away to college in the coming fall. She was not certain she could bear that.

As he took her arm firmly, she looked up at him, and her customary smile returned. It was best not to fill one's head with illusions of the future, which may or may not happen. Nor was it wise to dwell on the past, which is already written and cannot be changed. The present is all that can be controlled, and the present for Marie was very happy. More importantly, there was not a doubt in her mind that God would always give consolations to balance out the times of hardship to those who willingly suffer for Him. That was the source of her hope.

After a few more blocks, as they prepared to part, Thomas asked Marie if she was coming over to the Clarke house on Sunday, and she said that she was. A warning then was issued that Kathleen had been begging her parents to let her see the latest Harry Potter movie. They were trying to push her toward *Madagascar: Escape 2 Africa* instead. Even though going to the movies could be expensive, John Clarke enjoyed taking his daughter, and he did not want her to know anything about the state of the family's finances. Because Marie had read all the Harry Potter books, Kathleen was going to try to enlist her aid as a parental lobbyist.

"I enjoyed the last book, but it does have some intense and scary parts that are probably too much for her. I will be diplomatic."

"One mention of scary is all you need to say, though some groundwork should be laid down so that she won't be too disappointed. I will let you know how successful I am, and I will let you know how things go tonight."

"Are you really going to a party at Rex Burger's house?"

"I know, I know," Thomas replied. The post-game Friday night blowouts at the Burger household had become infamous. Mr. and Mrs. Burger would head out to their favorite watering hole and leave the house to Rex, Steve, and a hundred of their closest friends. These parties usually lasted until three in the morning. The football team members who went would drag themselves into school on Monday and try to outdo one another with stories of their debauched revelry.

Looking exhausted, pale, and sickly, they would inevitably end their weekend recap by stating how much money they had wasted and how bad they felt from their horrible hangovers. Thomas never attended any of these soirees, and his teammates would give him some good-natured teasing about it but not too much. Even though Rex was team captain de jure, Thomas was the captain de facto. His hard-nosed play on the field spoke for itself, but he was still considered lacking in machismo for not going to the parties. It was difficult for him to understand the bizarre notion of manliness that equated being an out-of-control, ignorant, crude, vulgar, drunken buffoon with being a man. A drunken buffoon is a drunken buffoon. Why would anyone aspire to that in life? No parent would want that for his or her child. And why, after disgracing yourself, your parents, your family name, and your ancestors back to the beginning of time, would anyone brag about it?

"I believe there is a big difference between fun and happiness," Thomas said to Marie. "It is possible to have both at the same time but only if reason is in command. These guys only seem to care about having disordered fun, an instant and constant satisfaction of their passions and sensual desires. I am sure they would say it is fun to do these things, but these actions only make them miserable and unhappy in the long run. This desire for fun controls them completely, and every week it seems like they need to do more and more ridiculous nonsense to get any enjoyment out of it at all, which ultimately only makes them more miserable. I prefer a long, peaceful life of freedom and happiness to one of enslavement to short-lived fun. Only virtue brings happiness, peace, and freedom."

"If I recall correctly," Marie retorted, "there was plenty of that nonsense going on at St. Titus as well."

"Unfortunately, that is true. I have noticed, though, that when you talk to anyone of these guys individually, whether at St. Titus or at West Ridge, he will privately admit how foolish it is to act this way, but when you get him in a group, he is afraid to admit it in front of the others." Thomas refrained from using the word "coward," even though it was appropriate. "Well, this is the life they have chosen for themselves. As Richard would say, trying to convince them to change would be like trying to teach a horse to speak Russian."

"I am sure Richard would be flattered to know that you are now including him in the list of people whom you quote," Marie replied.

"I have to admit that he does come up with a good one now and again."

The police had shown up the previous weekend as Mr. and Mrs. Burger were returning home, and the police officers told them in no uncertain terms that if there was one more wild party, the parents were going to jail. Thomas had been assured by many that Mr. and Mrs.

Burger would be home tonight to chaperone and that the party would only be a small gathering for the football team to celebrate the end of the season.

Thomas did not care much for Rex, but he did feel some pity when he saw an encounter between Rex and his father after the last West Ridge victory. Rex had played his best overall game and had been instrumental in defeating a very good team. When the young coaches took over, it took a while for Rex to get on board with the team concept. But eventually he did, and he had made a tremendous amount of progress as a player. The coaches went out of their way to commend him for it, but Mr. Burger did not see it that way. During the game, Stan Burger sat in the stands by himself, wearing a Fire Department baseball hat, sweater, and jacket; downing a flask; and yelling at the coaches. After the game, he staggered down to the field and hit Rex in the head violently, berating him in front of everyone for not carrying the ball more and telling his son how disappointed he was with him. After that, Thomas decided to be more patient with Rex.

When the invitation was offered for the get-together tonight, Thomas accepted. Athletes can come to a certain understanding with one another over a long season. Even though a team member may not like or want to be friends with someone he or she plays with, there is a respect given when seeing that person working hard and struggling for the team to succeed. Also, tonight very well could be the last time Thomas saw many of his teammates. Marie understood, but she was still wary and warned him to be careful.

"I promise, Marie. I will see you on Sunday."

***

A few hours later and after a three-mile walk, Thomas turned the corner onto a handsome street full of vintage

Chicago bungalows, all with neatly kept lawns. Except for one. The Burger manse, clearly of recent construction, filled up every square inch of the lot. There was no front lawn and no backyard; there was only a gigantic, three-story eyesore sticking out violently a quarter of the way down the block. The exterior of the home was gray cinder block mixed with inexpensive, loud yellow fascia brick.

When the neighbors found out about the plans for the teardown of the pleasant old home, they put up a vigorous yet futile battle to have it stopped. Mr. Burger had made a significant campaign contribution to Alderman Stein, and the zoning change sailed through the city council unopposed. Stan had been confident the alderman would come through for him because it was the same method he used to earn his "merit" promotion on the fire department.

Thomas could see people moving about behind the curtains, and even up close by the window, he heard only faint, muffled music. Everything appeared to be all right, so he ascended the stairs and rang the doorbell. No answer. He rang it again. Nothing. There was a dark, semicircular camera above the door, and he waved to it. Someone fiddled with the lock, and the door flew open suddenly.

The initial blast of ear-splitting rap music, which hit Thomas and forced him to take a step back, was directly followed by a huge plume of marijuana smoke. Someone grabbed his arm and pulled him inside. The door slammed shut behind him. It took a minute for Thomas to recover his senses and get his bearings. The bass from the music was pounding into his chest painfully as he looked around to see a house swarming with mostly young people but very little furniture. He rubbed his eyes and turned toward the dining room only to have someone slap a whiskey bottle in his hand, right before Desiree and Monique came stampeding toward him. Yelling incomprehensibly, they stumbled over each other and careened forward wildly.

Flashing lights were going off in the living room as Monique slammed hard into Thomas on her way to the ground, sending the whiskey bottle flying and almost knocking him off his feet. She made a feeble attempt to get up before falling down to the floor with a thud and passing out, totally immoveable. Thomas managed to stay on his feet as Desiree came at him next. With a strenuous amount of effort, he caught her and helped her collapse into a chair. He made his way to the next room and, hopefully, to an exit.

Parked at the kitchen table filled with half-empty red plastic cups and next to a keg of beer were Jeff Loder and Brian Kilbis, otherwise known in these situations as "J-Lode" and "Sleepy B." After clearing out space on the table and somehow managing to pull a huge bong out of nowhere, J-Lode looked over at the stranger who had just come in from the other room, smiled, and slowly pumping his fist said, "Yeah, what's up, bro? You want a hit?" Sleepy B. responded to no one in particular with a peace sign, a weak smile, and a heavy-eyed nod of the head as Thomas slipped out of this nightmare through the back door, into the gangway and freedom.

CHAPTER 15

Boy, this time it was hard. It could be one of a million things. Thomas racked his brain, trying to figure out why he found himself on the way to a tête-à-tête in the principal's office once again. He had made a game out of it by now, and his guesses recently had been right on the money. But today was different. Mr. Robert St. Pierre was most certainly the general cause for this summons, but what could it be specifically? So many things had occurred in the four days since Thomas's last visit.

In response to the students' repeated references to the upcoming Christmas holiday, Mr. St. Pierre had taken the offensive and declared boldly that he only believed in physical things. If he could not see it, touch it, taste it, hear it, or smell it, he refused to believe in it. The instructor then hurried over to his desk, pulled out a piece of paper, and proudly read, "To quote Cicero, 'If I am wrong in this, I am happy to be wrong. I don't want to give up my error as long as I live.'" Thomas pointed out most temperately, and almost with regret, that Cicero's statement was actually made in reference to the immortality of the soul. The proud smirk on Mr. St. Pierre's face dropped immediately.

Thomas then went on to explain that if a person only believed in things experienced through the senses, then that person would live in a world where the mind and the intellect did not exist, nor did logic or reason. None of those things could be seen, touched, tasted, heard, or smelled. More importantly, that person would also live in a world without truth, goodness, beauty, love, or life itself. A world without life, existence itself, would be a world devoid of reality, of what is.

Before Mr. St. Pierre could respond, Richard quickly surmised, "If that's the case, then Mr. Robespierre lives in a world of lies, evil, ugliness, hatred, and death, and the fact that he lacks a mind would explain the unreasonableness of his statement."

The teacher was fuming, unable to respond, when an idea hit William like a thunderbolt. He proclaimed excitedly, "That's what Lord Byron was talking about." Flipping through a book to return to a poem that had been assigned the week before, he read out loud:

"The beings of the mind are not of clay; essentially immortal, they create and multiply in us a brighter ray and more beloved existence: that which Fate prohibits to dull life, in this our state of mortal bondage, by these spirits supplied, first exiles, then replaces what we hate; watering the heart whose early flowers have died, and with a fresher growth replenishing the void."

As William closed his book with a look of profound insight, Richard looked back at "Mr. Robespierre" with a devilish grin and asked as innocently as possible, "Are there unicorns in the fantasy world you live in, too?"

Thomas had learned through the grapevine that after that exchange in class, Dr. Diaz received numerous calls from the parents of AP/Honors students. They wanted to know why their children had not been given the same classes that Thomas Clarke had. Why did he get some special information that their children did not? Why could he speak of things in class that their children had never been taught and had never even heard of before? Was there some conspiracy going on here to prevent their children from succeeding?

That certainly was one possibility why he was being summoned to see Dr. Diaz. Another could be the paper Richard had written on allegory and had turned in two days ago. "Mr. Robespierre" had refused to grade it and said he was going to talk with the principal first. Thomas had read over a copy of Richard's paper:

There were a hundred people in a room, having a discussion. At one point, someone declared, "One plus one equals two." Everyone looked around and agreed that this was true. After many, many years of saying that 1 + 1 = 2 is true, one person decided to disagree. He said, "One plus one does not equal two. One plus one equals three." Everyone else in the room did not know how to respond to this statement because it was obvious that 1 + 1 = 2. So, at first, no one paid much attention to this nebbish.

As time went by, this one irritating person kept insisting that 1 + 1 = 3. Day in and day out, year after year, it was repeated that 1 + 1 = 3. Then, amazingly, some other people began to accept it also. The overwhelming majority tried to explain that 1 + 1 = 2, not 3. If you have one apple in one hand and another apple in another hand, and then you bring them together, you end up with two apples, not three. The dissenter said in reply, "No, you are wrong. I don't care what you say. Your method of arithmetic is incorrect. One plus one equals three is a true statement."

Now the more able and educated stepped forward and tried to explain. Truth does not depend on our convoluted notions of logic, nor does it originate from any human being. We are not its author, nor its creators. It exists in and of itself. Something is true because it is in accord with Truth itself. One plus one equals two is not true because we say so. It is true because of what we know about Truth itself. Truth is whole and complete, lacking in nothing, deficient in nothing. It is perfect and will never change. It is eternal. One plus one equals two always has been true, is true right now, and always will be true. It does not matter if you accept it, agree with it, believe it, or understand it. The Truth was, is, and always will be.

The self-centered, fat-headed dissenter countered that he was being oppressed and discriminated against. The majority could not force their values on him and make him think like they did. He had rights. Furthermore, he would determine what was true, good, and just for himself. He would set his own moral limits—or not—and demanded that a law be put in place to ensure these rights.

Then, when anyone tried to respond, they were cut short with loud, irrational cries of "Bigots! Why do you hate people different from you? I obey the law. I pay my taxes. I am a good person. I put my life on the line for this country serving in the military. What difference does it make to you if I believe 1 + 1 = 3? How does that hurt anything in your life? Why can't there be a law that says I am the same as everyone else?"

Richard's reasoning was sound, even if the tone of the paper was overly confrontational, and he had obviously picked up on the Platonic themes that Thomas had spoken of before. In the last few paragraphs, which Thomas did not read, the conclusion was a thinly disguised attack on Mr. St. Pierre's chosen lifestyle.

Those were the leading candidates, and Thomas was fairly certain he could place his bets on them. But then again, there had never been any fallout, officially, from Dr. Diaz about the Burger household's end-of-season football party. Pictures had managed to show up on the Internet a few days after. Most were blurry and badly out of focus, except for two that clearly showed Rex and Steve wearing West Ridge football T-shirts and sweatpants while holding bottles of liquor and cups of beer. Dr. Diaz was about to come down hard on everyone who had been there when Rex frantically stated, "Thomas was there as well. Why isn't he getting in trouble too?" That put Dr. Diaz in a corner and added a whole different dimension to the situation. With the support of his parents, Steve Souter eventually came forward and confessed the real reason behind the party.

Stan Burger had taught his son that the world owed their family certain things, such as a high level of success in life. And when that success did not come as they expected it to, something or somebody else was always to blame—never them. Usually for the Burgers, the monster or boogieman that held them back was any combination of the government; blacks, Jews, and other minorities; the banking industry; big business; Wall Street; the church; or the school system.

In this instance, Mr. Burger had been certain that Rex was going to get a full scholarship to West Arkansas Technical University. That certainty was based only on the fact that the university had not asked Mr. Burger to stop sending them video of Rex's game play the way every other school had. They had no need to because the small state school had dropped their football program three years earlier for lack of funding. To Stan and Rex Burger, though, along with the usual suspects, it was also Thomas's fault that the scholarship fell through and that there were no other scouts watching Rex. (In reality, there had never been any scouts watching Rex.) Also, Rex had grown tired of hearing his inamorata gush on and on to her girlfriends about the quarterback and not about the running back. So a plan was hatched to destroy Thomas's chances of getting into college.

Even though the police had clearly warned about another blowout, the house had been put into foreclosure months ago, and the Burger family was leaving in two weeks. They had nothing left to lose. They had spent themselves into oblivion, and now everything had been taken from them. Even the beloved Tahoe had been repossessed. But if they could get Thomas Clarke on camera at the party, then at least he would share some of their misery.

Stan Burger and his lovely wife were indeed present at their home when it was filled with the potent mixture of alcohol, cannabis, and teenagers. Instead of waiting at his assigned spot in the living room with the camera, Mr. Burger gave in to his weak nature and began, early on, to imbibe in the various exotic delicacies on hand. By the time Thomas arrived, Stan Burger could barely stand. When Rex yelled at him to take the pictures, Thomas had been engulfed by the hair of Desiree and Monique. The digital camera was dropped, stepped on, and broken, but not before it fired off a burst of pictures, capturing clear images of the people in the living room. Steve finished recounting this pathetic tale by emphasizing that Thomas had been deliberately lied to and deceived and by admitting that Thomas had only been at the party for a minute or two at the most.

Dr. Diaz never actually saw a picture of Thomas on the Internet. There were a few with a young man in the background wearing properly fitting khaki pants and a light blue button-down shirt, a solitary figure in a sea of dark, loose fitting denim. But whoever it was, this person had been completely obscured from the chest up by what appeared to be two wild animals.

For his honesty, Steve served a week of in-school detention, while Rex was quietly suspended for two weeks. The incriminating pictures had been taken down off the Web, and Dr. Diaz prayed that the entire incident would blow over unnoticed and simply fade away. Thomas had told his parents the entire story of what happened at the party, and if Dr. Diaz had asked, Thomas would have told him the same. But nothing was ever mentioned about it. The Clarke family held no hard feelings toward Rex and his family.

That situation was another strong possibility for why Thomas was about to open the principal's office door on a Friday afternoon less than a week before Christmas. No matter. After this meeting was finished, he would go to the AP/Honors Club for an abbreviated session and then enjoy a much-needed vacation until the new year.

As he was about to say hello to the secretary, she

immediately picked up the phone and Dr. Diaz came out quickly with a serious look on his face. He said, "Mr. Clarke, I just received a call from your mother. She would like you to come home right away." Confused, Thomas looked over at Charlene Wilson, who tried to return a reassuring smile, then back at Dr. Diaz. "Just go now, Mr. Clarke."

CHAPTER 16

As Thomas made his way home, his disciplined mind refused to give in to groundless conjecture or, God forbid, despair. His mother called the school and asked him to come home. That was unusual, but no other information had been given. He assured himself, *It is not only in disordered loves but also in empty fears that all disquiet of the heart and distractions of the mind find their origins.* And thus, on this gray, overcast, and blustery afternoon, reason and love would again command Thomas Clarke's soul.

The family's old Saturn station wagon was pulling up in front of the house as Thomas turned the corner. His mother got out of the driver's side and hurried over to the passenger's side, where the door opened and a pair of crutches emerged. Thomas ran up and saw his father, looking more embarrassed than anything, struggle to exit the vehicle and make his way inside. A soft cast covered his father's right foot and extended halfway up to his knee, and Thomas noticed a large welt over his father's left eye.

"I'm fine. I'm fine," John repeated as his son came under his right shoulder and helped him limp through the front door. He plopped down on a large, cushy chair next to the piano and got himself situated. Margaret Clarke, still wearing her heavy coat and with her purse on her shoulder, stood over her husband. She gave him a soft smile of gentle concern. After fiddling with the crutches and finally setting them down on the side of the chair, John looked up at her and said reassuringly, "I'm okay. I'm fine. Go and get Kathleen from school." When she hesitated, he smiled and repeated that all was well. Margaret gave her son a quick glance, then kissed her husband vigorously on the top of the head before heading out the door.

"Tom, pull up a seat, will you?" John said as his embarrassment returned. As Thomas grabbed a chair from the dining room table, John noticed in his son the same calm demeanor mixed with a look of concern that his wife had shown in the emergency room and on the car ride home.

"Son, I am fine. I really am. What happened was I slipped on some ice in front of the shop and twisted my ankle pretty good. Then, as I fell, I smacked my head on the wall of the building and got this bump on my forehead. I am glad nobody was there because I am sure I looked like an idiot doing it." When his father laughed at himself, the stoic expression on Thomas's face broke into a smile. "There is no concussion or anything like that. I am going to have to wear this thing on my foot for about six weeks, though. So, like I said, I am going to be fine." Then his father wore a pained expression on his face, but it was not from his injuries. "There are some things I need to talk to you about, and I am glad we have some time here alone to do it."

John explained that the reason he slipped on the ice was because, as he walked up to the print shop, he became light-headed. The doctors ran a battery of tests and determined that his heart was fine and that he was generally in good health. He had not been eating right nor getting enough sleep. Months of stress and exhaustion had taken their toll, and those were caused by the financial state of the family business. But no more. John and Margaret had had a long discussion at the hospital and in the car. It was actually a continuation of things they had been talking over for some time, namely that John was not going to worry about things that were beyond his control. Margaret had been right all along. He had been wound up way too tight, and as a result, his health had suffered. It took a dramatic event like this for him to really understand that it was not worth it. His family needed him, and they meant too much to him.

His father paused for a moment, and Thomas listened intently as John continued, "So, that being said, I have decided to sell the print shop building." A look of anguish came over John's face as he said this. "Tom, I want you especially to understand why I decided to do this."

"Dad, you don't owe my any explanation. If you think it is best to sell the building, then so be it."

"No, no," John repeated insistently. "I have been telling you from the time you were little how important it is for people to set down roots where they live, how important it is for people to say 'This is my home, and this will be my home for generations to come, no matter what.' I have told you that a million times, just as my father used to tell me. You've heard the stories about how your cousins in Ireland have lived on the same rocky patch of land for thousands of years, in good times and in a lot of bad times as well. They certainly never had much. And even though it was far from perfect, they could pass on the farms from one generation to the next, and that would provide some kind of livelihood for their children to get by. That is what your grandfather wanted to do here, and that is what I wanted to do as well." The frustration in John's voice was rising, so he took a minute to calm himself.

"Tom, I don't know what exactly happened, but it has become impossible for a middle-class family to live and work in this neighborhood and in this city. I don't understand it. I am sure you have seen the way things have changed around here just in your lifetime. This neighborhood has gotten worse over the past twenty or thirty years, and I don't see an end to it. The increase in crime is frightening enough. It's not as bad as other parts of the city, but I don't want your mom and sister walking down the street alone. Tom, you know I am not a guy who sits around talking about glory days, but when I was a kid in this neighborhood, there was no crime around here at all. None. The city was corrupt then, just as it is now. The population in West Ridge was half Jewish and half Irish or German, and everyone could walk to Devon Avenue and get whatever you needed. And they could do it safely. There were grocery stores, clothing retailers, restaurants, bakeries, delis, toy stores, and movie theaters. You name it, it was there. No family at St. Titus had a lot of money, but an average Joe could afford to get married, buy a home and a decent car, send his kids to Catholic school, and still have enough to take a vacation once in a while. Now there is nowhere to shop, and there are no jobs around here. No one can open up a business either. People stay in their house nearly all the time. They hop in a car and drive miles to go to work or to buy whatever they need, and then they go back home again. A lot of people try to buy everything over the Internet, with minimum social interaction. There is no neighborhood here anymore. There are no real neighborhoods anywhere in Chicago anymore. I don't get it." John was getting red faced and exasperated, so his son tried to give him a breather.

"I know what you mean, Dad. People moved into this neighborhood and paid a lot of money—way too much—for a regular house, as if it was a palace. You would never see them around the neighborhood. They stayed for a few years, then moved someplace else. Those people have a different perspective on 'home' than we do."

John regained his composure and said, "That's right. A young married couple today just starting out would have to pay $800,000 for a two-flat or $500,000 for a simple bungalow. And that's not including the property taxes. Nobody can afford that. That's why the school and the parish closed. That's why so many families moved out to the suburbs. The only middle class left here are old people, like myself, and some city workers who are forced to live in the city. Once we start dying off, and this neighborhood has nothing left to offer anyone, what decent person is going to live here? I hoped that either you or your sister would get this house and never have to pay a mortgage. And I haven't really talked to you about it before, but I wanted you to have this business and the building with it. Now, though, I don't know what kind of future you and your sister will have." John stopped for a moment and reflected on everything he had revealed to his son.

"But, like I said, there is nothing I can do about most of that stuff, and I am not going to let it get to me anymore." His faced brightened up as he continued, "Your grandfather had to leave his home, come here, and start new. He did all right. My brothers and sister all moved out years ago. Things happen. I got caught up in this crazy notion of the rugged individual who can do it all himself, you know, the lone cowboy pulling himself up by his bootstraps. It is a ridiculous lie. I need you, your mom, and your sister. I do. Most of all, though, I have learned that you have to accept that there are things beyond your control, and you have to have enough faith to leave those things in God's hands. To have courage and hope, as I've heard people say around here. Even though nothing has been officially signed yet, I accepted an offer on the building for $900,000."

Thomas was shocked when he heard that number. "Really?"

"Don't think I am some great real estate guru. The same guy offered me $1.2 million six months ago, and I turned him down," John said with a resigned smile. "It's crazy. The building is not worth half that much, but if they are willing to offer that much right now, I have to take it. I will never get that much money for the property ever again. Look, we could make it through the winter and probably into next summer. After that, I don't know. I have never seen things this bad in my life. I would much rather keep the business and the building together, but I simply cannot get any loan from any bank anywhere. So, here we are. These developers want to tear down our building and the one north of it and put up four stories of condos above two commercial units on the first floor. They would give us the first choice of buying or leasing one of the commercial units if we want. In between now and then, Hans will let us use some of his space until the new building goes up and we figure out what we are going to do."

John was exhausted after that discourse. Thomas had never seen his father so distraught. His decision to sell the building clearly had been a difficult one. It was upsetting for Thomas to see, but he also felt the joy and pride only received by a son whose father was good, loving, and honorable.

"Dad, I know how much this means to you, and I realize how much it meant to Grandpa as well. I remember him telling me that his brothers and sisters in Ireland would tease him, calling him a 'tycoon' and referring to this house as 'the Mansion in Chicago.' But I know that they were proud of him, of how hard he worked for us and for them. Dad, whatever you decide, I have no doubt you are doing what is best for us all. Let me know what you need from me, and you've got it." A hug was requested and given.

"You are a good man, Thomas, the best I know," John said with pride. "Until everything is official, your sister doesn't need to know about this." Thomas nodded in agreement, and his father continued, "After all the legal stuff and the taxes are taken care of, the money still might not come for a while, and what remains will not be anywhere close to $900,000. Still, we are going to have to take a long, hard look to find the best place to set up next. I want you to help me with that." Thomas nodded again. "It's going to be expensive to move everything and get things going again, but there should be a little cushion left over that we don't have now. I don't need to tell you that things have been slow. And, as a result, Christmas this year might be a little scaled back. I'm sorry." John became visibly upset again.

With a smile of genuine happiness that surprised his father, Thomas quickly responded, "You know, Dad, the Church Fathers were described as being poor in earthly things but opulent in grace and virtue. Besides the great gift of suffering that we are receiving now, on Christmas morning, God will give the world the greatest gift ever: Himself. It would be prideful and presumptuous of me to ask for anything more."

John Clarke's head dropped and remained still for a long moment. He looked up with a wide grin, and then he generously doled out a loving, heartfelt hug.

CHAPTER 17

The Latin word for "door," *ianua,* comes from the name Janus, the Roman god of transitions and beginnings, also of doorways and gates. Janus had two faces, one looking forward and one looking back. The month of January, from *ianuarius* in Latin, was a time of one door closing on the old year and one door opening to the new, a period of transition where Old Man Time is replaced by Baby New Year.

At West Ridge Prep, the start of 2009 did not offer all that much change from the end of 2008. The nation and world were still tottering on the brink of financial destruction. Here, though, the school days quickly returned to their regular routine, with both students and teachers alike tossing aside last semester's syllabi with a sense of accomplishment while trying to find the strength to dig into the new ones.

Winter was entering its two most bitter and frigid months. There was nothing to be done about that except to endure it as bravely as possible. For the underclassmen, January felt so far removed from the end of the school year in June—but not for the seniors. There was an electricity that accompanied the beginning of their last high school semester, offering a mix of excitement, fear, anticipation, and hesitancy.

For Richard McGee, nothing was more thrilling than returning from the winter break and finding out that "Mr. Robespierre," with his unique powers of elocution, would not be returning to elucidate the deep mysteries of English literature for the spring semester. It was like a dream come true, although it also meant Richard would have to shelve the plans he had been working on to antagonize the instructor. He decided that it was for the best, admitting to himself that his severe case of senioritis would probably have led him to go too far. He glided into homeroom and told the others the good news with the joy of a condemned man gaining a last-second pardon.

"Has a replacement been named?" William asked in his usual serious tone.

"Billy, lighten up. The Wicked Witch is dead, okay? You know, I found out that liar only had an honorary PhD from some godless communist institute of higher learning in the Soviet Socialist Republic of Vermont. And that his 'published' thesis was actually 'published' on his own blog! To answer your question, though, Ricky Diaz has not named anybody yet. Whoever it is, he or she will be a large improvement from what we had." Richard was bursting with elation and could not believe that the others were not more enthusiastic about his news. No one had liked Mr. St. Pierre.

He looked over at Thomas, with Marie next to him. They were calmly taking it all in. Plato and Socrates suddenly came to Richard's mind, and he recalled how they urged control of emotions lest emotions control an individual. Richard took a moment to collect himself before quietly stating, "Pardon me, William. I spoke in haste. If we are patient, we shall learn shortly how Dr. Diaz intends to deal with this predicament." He walked over and sat down next to Thomas, who watched with an astonished smile. Richard had finished reading Plato and had started into Aristotle, but Aristotle was too dry. Putting that off until later, he shifted to Homer and Sophocles. At least there were blood and guts aplenty in Homer.

"You never know how deeply your vices have planted their roots in you until you try to pull them out and replace them with virtues. It is really hard," Richard confessed as he sat down with a grimace. His new hobby, fencing, had begun the night before, and it had been more physically demanding than he had anticipated.

Thomas commended him and encouraged him to fight on by saying, "Be brave. Remember, the Temple of Delphi proclaimed not only moderation but self-knowledge. If you try to do it on your own and without prayer, you will fail. But if you ask in faith for God's grace and strive to persevere, it will get easier. Eventually, you will conquer yourself and gain the upper hand."

When asked how his vacation had been, Richard replied with a shrug. His father had taken his entire family skiing in Colorado for Christmas. The beautiful house they had rented, described more than once as a "chalet," was close to the best lifts at the resort. Charles McGee's law firm, which specialized in tax law, zoning, and bankruptcy, had been doing very well recently. Richard and his mother flew out together. His older sister Laura, her husband, and their two young girls flew out the day after. Mr. McGee and his oldest son, Charles Jr., drove there in the enormous family Cadillac. Richard was happy to have his entire family together for the holiday, although he and his mother preferred a simple and smaller celebration to the grandiose. That's not what was bothering him, though.

"I heard your brother, Chuck, is going to work for your dad. Good for him. Tell him I said congratulations," Thomas said.

"Yeah, he finally managed to pass the bar on his third try. I don't know. There is something going on with him. He is upset that my dad is making him work his way up from the bottom, but it's more than that. He was acting weird the whole vacation, and it was making my mom upset too. At least he didn't bring his annoying girlfriend along this time." Richard quickly snapped out of his doldrums. "I can't complain, though. The skiing was great, the mountains were incredible, and it was nice to be with everyone for Christmas."

Except for Richard's sister and her family, the others all drove back in the Caddy. It only took a few days, and they took some pleasant back roads through various small towns. "Please don't misinterpret what I am about to say," Richard said with a wicked look in his eye. "Those small towns were beautiful, quaint, and picturesque. I enjoyed visiting them very much. The people were kind, hospitable, and generous. But, just so you know, if anyone ever goes to visit one of these small towns and expects it to be like the ones you see on television and in the movies, where everyone is young, prosperous, and good looking, it just isn't that way in real life. Wow." Richard caught himself before getting carried away again and cleared his throat. "I am sorry. I was simply trying to make an observation on the dismal state of the economy out in the rural areas and how incorrectly it can be portrayed in some parts of the media." Susan Donohue walked in, said "hello" in a very ladylike manner to the small group, and took her seat a few rows over. "If you all will excuse me, please," Richard said most politely and with a slight bow before moving over and sitting down next to Susan.

"I think she will be a very good influence on him, William," Thomas said.

"Indeed, my sister is very prudent in judgment and temperate by nature. We would all do well to emulate her more in these qualities. But Richard should be commended for the advancement he has made in overcoming some of the deficient aspects of his nature and manners," William responded dryly before returning to his studies.

"How is your father doing, Thomas?" Marie asked

when the two were alone.

John Clarke had not managed to master the use of his crutches, so he had been staying home, enjoying the much-needed rest. George was manning the shop, with Thomas going in to help him when needed. Business had been very slow over the holidays, and George had closed up early most days. Now that a few more orders were coming in and Thomas was going in after school, everything was under control, and John could recuperate at ease.

Christmas Day had made Mr. Clarke somber, but Kathleen noticed no difference in this holiday to any other. She had initially been horrified by the golf ball-sized lump on her father's forehead. It only got worse as the red welt shrunk and turned different shades of yellow, blue, purple, and green. But she got over that also and began to enjoy the rare treat of having her father at home for the entire Christmas break. The two spent so much time together that Margaret was afforded the luxury of being able to take care of her business for the day and still have some free time for herself. This bliss would not last forever, so they all took advantage of it while it lasted.

"My father and I have a meeting next week with the real estate developer. That is making him anxious, but overall he is much more relaxed and much more like himself. Thanks for asking. How is your mom holding up?"

Anne Martin had hosted her brother and his family for Christmas and worked hard with Marie to decorate their home and make a wonderful meal. Marie had noticed a slight change in her mother during this time, a little inkling of hope that would twinkle in her eyes as she put up the tree and looked over the old ornaments and pictures.

The evening started out most pleasantly with the children opening their presents before dinner was served. A magnificent, mouthwatering feast of roast beef, mashed potatoes, gravy, and green beans was served on the Martin family's finest china. Anne seemed very pleased and happy through dinner to do this for her family. Something in her wavered, though, during dessert. Marie could not figure out the cause, but her mother's emotions became unsettled. Despite everyone's efforts to continue the joyous mood, Anne began drinking and proceeded to make an embarrassing spectacle of herself. Uncle Frank and his family made a heroic effort to make the best of the situation, but they eventually had to leave earlier than usual. Marie put her mother to bed and cleaned up the mess. The rest of the night was spent in prayer.

When Anne got up for work the next morning, she went through her usual routine, quietly and slowly. One look at her, though, and anyone could tell that she was not feeling well. Marie came out to fix herself breakfast, and her mother stared at her with empty, sullen eyes. After what felt like an eternity for them both, Anne slowly walked up to Marie and wrapped her daughter in her arms. Tears were streaming down her face as she whispered in Marie's ear, "I'm sorry." The strong smell of alcohol reeked from the pores of her skin, but it was the first time after the deaths of her husband and mother that Anne Martin had ever expressed any regret for her actions to her daughter. It was also the first expression of concern and tenderness shown to her daughter in three years.

In the following days, Anne fell into a deep depression and remained withdrawn at home. Only in the last few days of Marie's vacation, her mother began to come around, and the mood in the house began to lighten.

"My mother wants to get better, and I know God will answer my prayers. We expect Him to be patient with us and our sins. We must be patient with Him and His grace. It will take time, but things are improving," Marie said with a confident smile.

Thomas took her hand and declared with his own smile of certainty, "If Richard McGee can become a gentleman, there isn't an atheist alive who can doubt that there is a God and that He still performs miracles."

CHAPTER 18

Dave Malone pulled into the parking lot of a sprawling shopping mall and checked the clock on his car radio and then on his cell phone. It was 8:55 a.m. He shut the car down and was surprised at how nervous he had suddenly become. His hands were shaking. A series of deep breaths stopped the tremors, but his stomach was still in a knot as his business partner, Ralph Bauer, pulled up next to him at precisely 9:00 a.m.

"Let's do this, man," Ralph said, barely containing his excitement.

"Yeah, let's go," Dave replied energetically. "We could be open for the Super Bowl."

"Wait, don't you mean 'The Big Game'?" Ralph replied with a laugh.

"Whatever."

The two young men were on a mission of grave importance to them and to their comrades. One of the oldest neighborhood bars in West Ridge, The Green Lantern, had been shut down by the city three weeks earlier. There were various code and zoning violations outstanding, but mainly, the previous owner had failed to stay current with the taxes and with various state and city licenses, owing various government revenue agencies close to $30,000.

Dave Malone worked downtown in the IT department of a finance company. Ralph Bauer, a plumber, had not worked at all in two months. Both in their late twenties and very eager, they had managed to work out a good deal where the government agreed to accept less than $8,000 from them to make restitution for the 900-square foot neighborhood icon. From the government's perspective, getting some revenue was better than getting none, but a four-month deadline was set to make things right. To get the city license, to clear out any zoning problems, and most importantly to fulfill their long-standing dream of owning a bar, the blessing and approval of Alderman Mordecai Stein was required.

The two young men were joking and backslapping each other as they entered the plain, second-floor office, which was tucked away in a remote corner of the mall. The empty waiting area meant things were only looking good. If they could get this meeting over with quickly, they could start ordering the liquor this afternoon and have everything stocked and ready to go for 'The Big Game' next week. Even though the game featured Pittsburg against Arizona, their second home would be back in business, with Malone and Bauer in charge now, dishing out drinks like it was their private frat house. After making a sizable profit at the new Green Lantern, they were also thinking about franchising around the Chicagoland area . . . and then the nation. The people who own the bars in Lincoln Park and around Wrigley Field are millionaires; the thought of what could be done nationwide was dazzling.

The two confidently walked up to the front desk and signed in. The office manager, a man about their age, came over and asked what the young entrepreneurs needed. They explained their situation, and the office manager replied with a strange question.

"Are you two here by yourselves?"

What was that supposed to mean? Of course, they were there by themselves. The office was empty.

"So you came on your own, and nobody sent you here?"

The revenue people from the state and the city said the alderman had to sign off on the paperwork, so those government employees sent them there.

"Hold on for a minute, please," the office manager said with an odd look before going into the back room and talking with a middle-aged, heavyset woman wearing a huge, shiny, black wig. The door to the back room remained ajar, and Malone and Bauer could see the woman quickly look up at them and shake her head. The office manager returned and stated that the alderman had meetings scheduled all morning. If the two would take a seat, the alderman would see them when a moment was freed up. Assuring themselves that it would not be a long wait, they turned around and looked for the most comfortable plastic chairs they could find.

By 3:00 p.m., Malone and Bauer had not eaten anything since breakfast. They sat, staring blankly at the same forty-year-old abstract art and at the ceiling, as broken men. Ralph Bauer meekly returned to the front desk and asked what the alderman's appointment schedule looked like for the rest of the afternoon. Booked up. Could they make an appointment for tomorrow? That was booked up too. They could either come back and wait tomorrow, or they could try again next week sometime. Their heads hung low as they accepted defeat and walked slowly out of the office.

What they did not know at the time was that after three months of this game, the alderman would finally grant an audience and offer his sincerest efforts to help them while making it clear how unfortunately expensive aldermanic elections had become. It was a shame. He was determined to help the two nice young men, but if he didn't get re-elected, they would have to start the whole process over again with someone new, and the new person may not want to help them. After a sufficient campaign contribution had been made, all their problems would disappear. But if the right person had sent them there in the first place, all of this unfortunate business could have been avoided. The game would be learned eventually, but today was a day of crushed dreams.

Mr. Choudhry, the owner of East-West Electronics and Luggage on Devon Avenue, had learned the lesson well many years ago and was shown directly into the back office. His problems with building code violations were taken care of within five minutes. The rail thin, middle-aged Pakistani man, dressed in a loose-fitting tunic and baggy pants, put on his winter coat while offering profuse thanks for the alderman's time and trouble.

"Gabby, check our records," the alderman ordered. "If everything is all right, give Said a call at the building department and straighten that out."

"I will."

"When is that husband of yours getting here? I have a dinner reservation at Myron and Phil's in a half hour."

"He's coming in now."

In a flurry, Sheldon Abramowicz threw off his heavy overcoat, gave his wife a kiss, loosened the tie that was strangling him, and adjusted his poorly fitting wrinkled suit before plunging himself uncomfortably into the chair in front of the alderman's desk. "Feh! Can't you give a person a decent place to sit down?" He opened his briefcase and took out a stack of papers.

"Ach, don't be a kvetsh. Seeing the size of you, I doubt there is such a decent chair in existence," replied the 350-pound alderman. "What news do you have for me?"

"Oy, nothing good," the president of Silver Screen Realty stated with disgust. "The condos on Ridge and Touhy Avenues, nobody wants them. We could not give them away if we wanted to. Same with the townhouses on Pratt and most of the apartment buildings and single-family homes. No one is buying anything. We have taken out ads in the neighborhood Hebrew papers to announce that all the prices have been reduced. Word should get around. We have to sell whatever we can quickly, even if we have to take a small hit on the price."

What a schlemiel my son-in-law is, the eighty-three-year-old Alderman Stein thought to himself. "Shelly, how many times have I told you, we can't try to sell these units to local people. They know how overpriced everything is. You have to sell to some schmuck from the suburbs, or from out of state. They don't know any better."

Sheldon Abramowicz did a slow burn, tired of hearing his father-in-law's repeated words of wisdom. "I have told you before, everyone in the business says this slowdown is only temporary."

"Listen to Mr. Real Estate Maven."

Shelly responded with increasing agitation, "The fact is that we have a big balloon payment coming up soon. We need sales. We need cash flow. Fast. Maybe you could get your friend Mr. Khan to have his bank lend us some more money? We can't get a loan to tear down the two buildings by the railroad tracks. First, he gives us the money to buy the buildings, and now he won't give us any more money to finance the construction. Tell me, what kind of shmendrik does that?"

"All right, don't have a plotz. I have done business with Mr. Khan for thirty-five years. I'll talk to him." The alderman's words did little to ease his son-in-law's worry. "Relax, Shelly, you're mishpocheh. We'll work it out."

***

"Are there any more questions?" Katie Sullivan scanned the room slowly. AP/Honors English had been thrust upon her by Dr. Diaz at the last minute simply because she had been the only English teacher with an advanced degree and open time in her schedule to take it. Her initial reaction was annoyance, then fear began to creep in. The academic reputation of these students was well known among the "regular" teachers. Taking over a class mid-semester, especially one of high-achieving seniors about to graduate, could shake any teacher's confidence.

Ms. Sullivan was twenty-eight years old with undergraduate and master's degrees in English from a small state school. Most AP teachers were much more experienced, possessed PhDs, and boasted much better pedigrees. She certainly was not imposing to behold; she was tall and lean, with a lithe and airy manner. Straight, chestnut hair pulled back in a ponytail, along with a pale complexion and a face full of freckles, made her appear much younger than she was. That caused her more concern as well. The reputation some of these AP/Honors students had for being tough on teachers was also well known.

The first chaotic days had been sorted out quickly, though, and the last few weeks had been very rewarding and had proceeded apace. These students were most capable. The class had definitely been a step up not only in the level of work and preparation required of her but also in the depth of the subject matter covered and the amount of effort she could expect from her students. She had met the challenge ably and professionally. Despite physical appearances, Katie Sullivan had some grit.

Richard had noticed that on the first day when she put Scott Weber in his place after Scott decided to test the seemingly frail lightweight with an arrogant comment. The matter was handled quickly and decisively, and Richard decided immediately that he liked this new teacher. She was smart as a whip and all business, a breath of fresh air. His battles with that other teacher were a thing of the past, and everyone in class appreciated the calmness that had settled in. As long as Scott Weber was around Richard, though, there would be some tension in the air. Even though she did not require it, Richard had appointed himself as Ms. Sullivan's protector for the rest of the year, and he intended to carry out his duties with distinction and vigor.

"Okay, if there are no more questions, I want to remind you that your papers on *The Tempest* are due next week. Thank you." She began to clear her desk, then turned back to the class with a note in her hand. "Mr. Clarke, could you come up here, please?" Ms. Sullivan felt it was unprofessional to address the students by their first names.

As Thomas approached, he asked with a knowing smile, "Dr. Diaz?"

"Yes. He would like to see you again."

It was difficult to understand. This was the fourth time in three weeks that Thomas Clarke had been summoned by the principal. He was clearly at the top of this class, very bright and incredibly hardworking, polite and cheerful, and not wound up like most of the others. Initially, it was not clear to Ms. Sullivan why the other students were so attentive when he spoke, but then it became obvious when he began to eloquently express deep and profound insights into literature, things even she had never thought of and things that only made her a better teacher. She knew he was a transfer student from a local Catholic school and that he was the big football hero a few months ago. So why was he always going to the principal's office, and why was she required to send updates on his progress and activities in class? She thought about asking him if everything was all right. A trip to visit Dr. Diaz was as popular as cleaning a bathroom, but Thomas Clarke seemed unconcerned, even happy at the news, so she let it go.

"Thank you, Ms. Sullivan." Thomas took the note and began the well-worn journey that he could now make with his eyes closed. At least he knew what this one was about. Because he had to work nights periodically at the print shop, he had missed the first two meetings for the Speech Club. Dr. Diaz was aware that John Clarke had been injured, and he could not fault Thomas for attending to family matters. Rather, it was the speech given the day before on diversity that was the cause of the poor principal's present perspiration and perplexity.

Thomas offered salutations to Ms. Wilson and was shown right in. Dr. Diaz had long since discarded with the pleasantries and told Thomas to sit down. After crossing his legs and making himself at home in the large, comfortable chair, Thomas looked up at his principal and said blithely, "Thank you, Dr. Diaz. What can I do for you today?"

Dr. Diaz picked up a copy of the offending speech and read it over, occasionally muttering to himself, "Okay, this part is good." He was referring to Thomas's description of the wide variety and diversity of what is good, just, and true.

Thomas had written:

We all must recognize and cling to the better and higher aspects of our natures. We must also recognize, that within the width and depth of humanity, there is an equally wide span of what constitutes that which is good and true in each person. That goodness may not always be easy to see, but it is there, no matter how faintly it may seem. We should all try to bring this goodness in ourselves and in others to the forefront, nurture it, and let it grow.

Then Dr. Diaz's shirt collar became drenched, and his brow furrowed. He muttered under his breath and began to read aloud:

"Even though there is a diversity of the good, by no means can a society embrace and condone that which is evil. The effects of evil may not be perceived by the senses, but they can be brought to light with the proper application of reason. The disordered society that clings to evil and vice dies away slowly but surely, convincing itself how progressive and modern it is in its thinking and how superior it is to all others. At the same time, such a society buries its head in the sand and shamelessly denies the obvious: the prideful man who turns into his imperfect, finite, mutable self rejects and separates himself from unchanging, perfect, and eternal Truth and Goodness. Wherever pride rears its ugly head, run away from it as far and as fast as you can. Pride leads one to desire what is dishonorable and to desire honorable things dishonorably as well. The natural consequences of unnatural pride are death and darkness, division among humanity, and separation from God, the source and summit of Truth and Goodness."

Dr. Diaz stopped reading and crumpled up the paper in disgust. He finally vocalized his thoughts by saying, "I can't use any of this stuff!"

In a morning press conference, the mayor had officially announced that the present superintendent would be stepping down at the end of the year and that a nationwide search would be undertaken to find a replacement. Ricardo Diaz had been told by his advisers that now was the time to make his greatest impression on the mayor—and with the biggest splash. The principal was counting on Thomas to deliver flowery and fluffy speeches with all kinds of impressive looking quotes that he could then take credit for and use to promote himself. He could only use a handful of these lines, but none of them were good enough to put in the school paper or the citywide newsletter.

"I want you to write this speech again." It was more of a command than a request.

"I am sorry, sir. Do you feel there is a deficiency in my reasoning? It would be my pleasure to discuss that with you." Thomas's customary easy manner was beginning to move beyond slight irritation for the aspiring principal and into the realm of excruciating annoyance, like bamboo shoots being jabbed under his fingernails. Thomas then asked innocently, "Is there any one part in particular that troubles you, sir?"

Dr. Diaz had read enough teacher reports to know that entering into a debate with Thomas Clarke would be a foolish endeavor. His anger rising, he merely repeated, "I need you to write a better speech on diversity."

Thomas thought for a moment before replying calmly, "I don't understand what that means, sir. I gave my best effort when I wrote this speech. I am certain there could be stylistic improvements in the presentation but not in the substance. Seeing as how this speech was for a school club presentation and not a grade, could you please clarify what you mean, sir?"

Dr. Diaz could swear there was a defiant expression on this kid's face and was about to erupt when the radio on his desk crackled to life: "Engineer Schmitt to Principal Diaz. Over." After a second without reply, the request came more urgently, "Engineer Schmitt to Principal Diaz. Over. We have a frozen pipe that burst and a major water leak in the library. You need to get down here right away."

The principal raged with fire in his eyes, and Thomas responded with complete passivity, "Will that be all, sir? It sounds like that emergency needs your immediate attention. I don't want to be a bother to you."

That put Dr. Diaz over the top, but the radio came to life, cutting in and out with the sound of gushing water and the frantic building engineer calling for help. It was like something from the last hours of the *Titanic*. Dr. Diaz snatched the radio in a fury and rushed out of the room. Thomas collected his things and graciously wished Ms. Wilson goodnight. He left the office and would not allow himself the slightest grin of victory. Only four and a half months until graduation, and it appeared that Dr. Diaz had finally had enough of these biweekly meetings. Patience is born when the cardinal virtues of temperance, fortitude, and wisdom are exercised properly. Once again, balance and order prove to be best in all things. Thomas put on his jacket, picked up his schoolbag, and went out front to walk Marie home.

CHAPTER 19

With the turning of time, the clouds parted, and the gray gloom began to lose its grip. Glimmering streaks of sunlight broke through the din and began to thaw the powerfully frigid cold and snow. The sun, it seemed, had not appeared since November, and its prolonged absence tempted one to believe that it was gone forever. The first days of February, though, offered a taste of the warmth to come and a welcome respite from one of the coldest Januaries ever. Winter was not yet fully prepared to retreat and cede all the ground that it had gained. Hebe, the Greek goddess of spring and of youth, was still confined in an icy cage. But if a hearty soul could bravely bear four more weeks of battle, the worst of the icy beast's assaults would be in the past. With each second, each minute, each hour, and each new day conquered, the hope of spring—and final victory—grew with them.

Marie stood at a second-floor window and stared out across a snowy field behind the school. In a short time, that field would be filled with budding flowers and green grass. The days were now sliding past quickly, tumbling one into another. While most everyone else had the end of school at the forefront of their thoughts, Marie was waiting for the university acceptance letters to arrive, letters that would provide some clarity about her future and Thomas's. Her thoughts were abruptly interrupted by a loud disturbance behind her.

Quickly making her way to the lunchroom, Marie was happy to find Thomas there alone, and she related the account of a disturbing event that had just happened to William in the hallway. Rex, sporting his new buzz cut hairdo, waited for William to close his locker, then slammed into him and knocked William's books all over the hallway. Steve Souter valiantly tried to stop Rex, but his efforts were to no avail. Steve gave up and walked away. Rex proceeded to scream furiously at William to be more careful, threatening dire consequences if his warning was not heeded.

William came up to the table and sat down, appearing none the worse for wear. He asked Marie for help to clarify a calculus problem.

"I will be happy to help you with that, but is everything all right?"

As William unwrapped his lunch, he replied, "Well, I must admit, apart from calculus, Spanish has been more challenging than I had anticipated. French came to me very easily, but for some reason, Spanish has not. Seeing as how they are both based on the Latin root, it is perplexing why one is more difficult than the other. Quite a conundrum actually."

Marie gave a concerned look to Thomas, who asked, "William, did you have some kind of trouble in the hallway? Are you hurt?"

"Are you referring to the mishap with Rex Burger? That was nothing, and I am not injured in any way."

"Did he threaten you?"

"Pardon me, Thomas, but why would anyone give credence to anything Rex says? I have learned from you that words are empty darts of air; they could not scratch a stone. I don't mean this to sound harsh, but Rex Burger is sorely lacking in cognitive ability. I have also surmised that he is essentially a coward. When we graduate in a few months, there is a very high statistical probability that I will never encounter Rex Burger again in my lifetime. That is, unless he sought to work for me in some capacity in the future. He is a very disagreeable fellow, though, and it is unlikely I would ever offer him a tender of employment," William answered while methodically laying out each piece of his lunch in its proper place.

"That is very prudent and very temperate, William."

"Considering the source, I take that as high praise. Thank you, Thomas."

Marie moved a few seats over to eat and discuss calculus as Richard came up to the table.

"Hey, Rich," Thomas ventured.

"Hey," Richard responded despondently.

"I heard your brother is getting married. Congratulations," Thomas said gently.

Richard stared at the table with a look of anger and resignation before replying bitterly, "I imagine everyone has heard by now. Thank you for being considerate." Charles McGee, Jr., Richard's elder brother by ten years, had impregnated his girlfriend. The rushed wedding was to be held in a few weeks. "My dad is furious, but my mom is a wreck. How could he do something like this to her?" Joan McGee was a very pious woman.

Richard had looked up to Chuck more than to anyone else. As a child, Richard was ecstatic whenever his older brother would hang out with him, and Chuck McGee was very generous with his time, teaching his younger brother how to ride a bicycle, field a grounder, and throw snowballs at CTA buses without getting caught. He would take Richard, Thomas, and their friends to Cubs games, joking with them and treating them as equals, not as little kids. At St. Titus, Chuck would go out of his way to say hello or come over to his brother in the hallway and talk with him for a second. In these little ways, Chuck let

Richard know his big brother was there and looking out for him.

Things changed when Chuck went to college and started dating Lisa, whom Richard and the rest of his family despised immediately. She was tall and lean, most likely an athlete, with bleach blonde hair, and she had quickly demanded most of her new boyfriend's time. Marie often questioned why any woman would want to dress like a man, but Lisa was more like one of the guys, having never been taught how to act in a feminine manner. The foul-mouthed, sharply tongued temptress lured Chuck into her web through the pleasures of alcohol and the flesh. Seven years later, after numerous breakups and reconciliations, Chuck and Lisa would finally reap what they had sown.

"Just when I start to make some progress with this virtue thing, this she-beast gets thrown in my face."

"Rich, have you ever seen how gold and some other metals are refined and purified?" Thomas asked.

"What?" Richard replied, annoyed.

"First, they have to go into a crucible of fire and intense heat to burn away the impurities, then the smith takes them out and pounds on them with a hammer to mold them. Either that or they let them soak in a bath of acid."

"So what?"

"Virtue is only refined and purified when it is put to the test in the crucible of suffering. There is no other way. You are not being punished here; you have been given a gift."

"Some gift. I'd rather have a plane ticket to Hawaii right now."

Marie returned and joined the conversation. "You are never given a test that you cannot endure and overcome." Richard looked at his two friends and bit his lip. They had suffered far more than he had. Marie continued, "What more perfect test could there be for you than to act with perfect charity toward the person you detest most in the world?"

"You know what gets me the most?" Richard was in agony and needed to vent. "Now, all of a sudden, she acts like little Suzy Homemaker, like we are all supposed to forget what a disgusting, drunken tramp she has been for the past seven years. Whenever she would watch a movie based on Charles Dickens or Jane Austen, she immediately identified herself with the aristocracy when, in reality, if she lived back then, she would have been changing the bedpans in a manor house, cleaning out the stalls of a barn, or working the streets. And she always wears this cross around her neck and puts on this nauseatingly false piety. Oh, she makes me sick to my stomach! I am so glad that little gold digger has gained at least forty pounds! She will look horrible in her wedding dress even if she tries to hide the disgrace of the circumstances! She is one of those people who never reads anything and is constantly on her smartphone Googling whatever is being talked about and then making moronic little comments about things she doesn't know anything about. That's what the United States has been reduced to: a nation of scatterbrained idiots who scan a few lines on the Internet and think that makes them an expert on everything. Whoever said that a little bit of knowledge is a dangerous thing was right." He paused and continued morosely, "And yet, she is going to be my brother's wife, mother to his child, and a part of my family. Christmas from now on should be so pleasant."

"Richard, let me tell you this," Marie said tenderly. "No matter how rough her exterior may be, the maternal instinct in every woman is very strong and can lead to a great metamorphosis in character. At the same time, though, the love of a mother for her child must be nurtured. You love your brother and want him and his new family to be happy, don't you? Your example of virtue to him—and to the rest of your family—can help make that happen."

Richard reluctantly agreed, but he still needed to vent. "I simply cannot understand how any son could be so blind and selfish! How could he not see the grief and suffering his actions would bring to our parents? I will vow this: nothing in my life from now on will ever do that." His anger was now abated. "You know, I recently started to do the Morning and Evening Prayers in the Liturgy of the Hours. They have been helpful, and they're simple enough to do. They only take about ten minutes a piece. But reading *The Imitation of Christ* was like a punch in the gut. And now this!"

"You are on the right path, and forgiveness is part of it," Thomas reassured him. "The greater the trial, the greater the victory. Embrace this cross and offer it up. Marie and I are here to help if you need it."

Richard gave a slight nod and then sulked off in a depression.

"Marie, have you met Lisa?" Thomas asked.

"I have. Richard has a tough road ahead of him."

"Yes, he is going to need *a lot* of prayers to get through this."

***

An unusual silence came over the Clarke household, broken only by the sounds of John scampering around in a rush. The family had already said its Evening Prayer before dinner. Afterward, after everyone else had left, the dishes had been quickly washed and the kitchen swept and cleaned. The newspaper had been gathered up and put in the recycling bin. John had hobbled out to the garage, having ditched his crutches, to bring in some packages for his wife. Finally, he made a tall glass of ice water for himself and planted himself in front of the old RCA tube television with four minutes to spare. On this rare night home alone, John Clarke was blessed to enjoy—in complete privacy—two hours of the greatest television show ever made: *Magnum, P.I.*

He caught his breath and settled into the cozy cushions of his favorite chair, wrapping a blue-and-white wool blanket around his legs. He pushed the power button on the remote control, and the glow from the back of the TV set caused eerie shadows to form on the wall as the eighteen-year-old device warmed up and hummed to life. The 26-inch CRT screen finally crackled on just in time for the rugged theme song to blare out of the speakers and Tom Selleck to stick a pistol in his belt, jump in his red Ferrari, and speed off after the bad guys.

Margaret had volunteered in January to lead the Queen of Peace children's choir and tonight was the last rehearsal before they would sing at Mass on Sunday and then give a short performance afterward. Kathleen was happy to join the choir, especially since she would no longer be going to ballet. The lessons were too expensive, but John and Margaret were also very cautious about what activities and people their impressionable daughter would be allowed to participate in and surround herself with. They knew that nothing good was going to come out of her being around other children who were allowed—and even encouraged—to be willful and out of control. Vices implanted in the soul at such a tender age have the potential to set deep roots that could spread and do a lifetime of damage.

Kathleen got over her initial disappointment through participation in the school choir, her continued piano lessons, and helping her mother make a new dress to be worn at Thomas's high school graduation. Thomas had gone to the shop for a few hours and would be back soon.

Margaret made her husband promise that he would not go back to work full time until the doctor cleared him. The approval had been given that afternoon, and even though John had enjoyed his break and his time with his family, he was looking forward to getting back to the shop, especially now with so much uncertainty from the real estate people who had offered to buy the building. They had been very elusive about why the deal needed to be postponed temporarily. That would be dealt with tomorrow. Tonight would be spent wading into danger with private investigator Thomas Magnum.

He took a long sip of his refreshing drink and readjusted his blanket. John was amazed at the incredible picture quality. The recent announcement that the analog television signals would be replaced with digital ones initially caused alarm, but an inexpensive converter box hooked right into the antenna wire from the roof worked perfectly. There was no super high-definition signal. What came through, though, was incredible, and because of the large antenna attached to the chimney and the lack of tall buildings and trees nearby, over forty digital signals were being picked up from all over the area. A local Chicago station had dedicated three channels to airing old reruns, and tonight back-to-back episodes of *Magnum, P.I.* were coming in far better and clearer than when they originally aired.

As the second episode was coming to a close, Thomas returned from the print shop with some good news, but he was immediately hushed by his father. When a commercial came on, John apologized. "Sorry, Tom. This is a really good one. Magnum got hired by a Chinese antique dealer to protect her vase until she sells it. The episode's called "The Soul of Soong." But he has to battle this gang, the Tongs, and a Wing Chun martial arts assassin who are trying to steal the vase. Oh, wait, wait! It's coming back on."

As Thomas watched his father's rapt attention to the show's dramatic conclusion, it was good to see his dad back to his old self: relaxed, easygoing, humorous, and with a fanatical devotion to *Magnum, P.I.* As the credits rolled, John gave his studied comments, "That was an early one. It was good, though not as good as the two "Did You See the Sunrise?" episodes. However, it is strange that Magnum runs into some tough characters in this one, but he doesn't use his usual M1911 Colt .45. I never understood that."

"Dad, when are Mom and Kathleen coming home?"

"They should be home any minute. How did it go at work?"

"Very well actually. Mr. Stanton and I finished up the orders for today. They can ship tomorrow."

"That's great."

"And we got calls from Walgreens, the gas company, and a railroad company saying that they all want to enlarge their orders that we were going to start next week."

"It is good to hear someone's business is doing all right. That is good news for us as well."

"You may have heard this earlier today, but the other good news was that a fire inspector showed up this morning."

"No, I did not hear about that. How much is this good news going to cost me?"

"Well, Mr. Stanton showed him around, and the guy was done in ten minutes."

"It was a man?"

"Yes, a big, muscular, bald-headed black guy. Mr. Stanton said this inspector knew what he was doing and was very professional. He asked how business was going and said he wasn't there to hurt anybody, that he just wanted to make sure the building was safe. After this gentleman said everything was fine, Mr. Stanton showed him the old violation letter from last fall. The guy was very apologetic and said the woman who wrote those violations did not know what she was doing, and he promised that he would take care of it. He left his name and number if you want to call him tomorrow."

"That is good news," John replied with a relieved sigh. The phone number Bob Einhart had given him for the building department cleaned up that mess immediately. The Department of Revenue, though, forced Clarke Printing to buy a nonrequired hazmat license. The phone calls to the Fire Prevention Bureau were an effort in futility. A few civilians there appeared to be reasonable and knowledgeable, but the fire personnel were not. If this inspector could straighten things out, that would be a tremendous help.

Margaret and Kathleen came home. They felt tired but were in good spirits as well. Kathleen saw her father up and about without crutches for the first time in many weeks, and she gave him a big hug and a kiss before her mother put her to bed. When Margaret returned, she inquired if it was *Magnum, P.I.* alone that had put the smile on her husband's face and the spring in his step or if there was some other reason as well. When Thomas and his father relayed all the day's news, she gave her husband and son warm hugs and kisses. Margaret was grateful, happy, and relieved to hear anything positive at all. She had fought hard to ensure that love and hope would always be in ample supply and would keep their home warm. This news was trifling in the grand scheme of things, but it had been a long winter, and even the smallest slice of good news was long overdue. Solaced by the brief respite of one small victory in a very long campaign, they all turned in for the night and fell into a deep, restful sleep.

CHAPTER 20

The tension in the homeroom was heavy and mingled with hysterical panic, brewing up a lethal elixir of inconsolable despair and thoughts of irrational, desperate plans for surviving the pending day of national doom. For Scott Weber, and many who had made the fateful decision of listening to him, March 2009 was truly the end. They were not present at the birth of this great country in July 1776, but they would bear witness to its demise. Every bank in the country, the entire financial system, and the once-powerful United States of America itself were all clinging to their last desperate gasps of life, feebly trying to ward off the Grim Reaper from completing his inevitable and irrevocable task of death.

Scott would glance at his phone and read aloud that bank stocks were collapsing. Another person would quote the "Dow Jones Industrial Average massacre." Yet another worried openly about the "bleak hope for jobs to ever return." Scott then fell to his knees and began to bewail his overly dramatic tale of woe, followed by feigned calm acceptance. It was only a matter of hours now. Hopefully, the end would be quick. No one wants to see the suffering caused by a lingering, drawn-out death. Just as he had caught his breath from encouraging the others to accept their grisly fate, another scan of the phone and more news of historic selloffs, investor sentiment at record lows, and no end in sight caused another eruption of gloom.

"Without a loan from the bank, there is no way I can go to medical school," Scott said, hyperventilating. "There probably won't even be medical schools anymore. What am I going to do? Will I have to be a garbage collector or something like that? Oh, their uniforms are filthy, and they smell so bad! And there is no way I could ever afford to buy the really big BMW as a garbage collector. There probably won't even be cars anymore either."

As Scott paced the room, horrified and convinced that he would not last long in a world about to revert to a post-apocalyptic stone age, Richard sat calmly with Thomas and Marie.

"Not going to take the bait, eh?" Thomas asked.

Richard looked over at Scott, who was frantically attempting to decide if his slim chances of survival were better in a warmer climate, where there would be more people who were stronger than he was, or in a harsher, colder one with fewer people overall. At least the cold weather, Scott contended, could kill off some of the more exotic diseases certain to ravage the countryside.

"No," Richard replied simply. "As a wise man once said, 'You have accomplished nothing once you have bested a fool.'"

"Wasn't that Glen Campbell in *True Grit*?" Thomas asked.

"Indeed it was," Richard said while turning in his chair away from the cabal of doom. "Seriously, though, if you have never taken the time to learn in depth about finance, government, foreign affairs, national affairs, history, technology, and the law, I don't understand why anyone would want to have this mass of instantaneous information. What do most people need it for, and what do they do with it once they have it? If you don't understand anything about that stuff, it sure seems to do more harm than good."

Richard had made great strides in mastering his passions and acquiring a basic level of temperance. Before taking over the AP/Honors English class, Ms. Sullivan had been repeatedly warned specifically about Richard, but she had found him to be a model student, even gentlemanly at times toward her and toward the other students, especially Susan Donohue.

This newly found self-control had also made Richard a more fearsome opponent to others, namely Scott Weber. Where in the past Richard would begin to make a point and then quickly lose control, appearing foolish and comical, now his mind could focus on the weaknesses in an opposing argument and apply a devastating—and credible—response in a civil manner. Richard quickly saw the effectiveness of this tactic and doubled his efforts to master it.

"Come on, McGee!" Scott ran up and shouted, with eyes bulging and red from lack of sleep. "None of that Amero stuff. Just tell us what you know."

"I don't know, Scott. I don't have a smartphone," Richard replied casually.

"Look at this!" A smartphone was shoved two inches in front of Richard's eyes. "Do you know what this means?"

"No, I will read about it tomorrow in the paper. Excuse me."

The McGees had been longtime subscribers to the *Chicago Tribune* and *The Wall Street Journal,* but Richard never began to read them consistently until he gave up the Internet for Lent in mid-February.

"Actually, I was going to suggest reading the newspaper to him, but what is the point?" Richard surmised. "It really doesn't matter where some nitwit gets the news from because he can't understand it anyway. Even with limitless amounts of information at their fingertips, most people don't know what the Bill of Rights is or what is in it. They could not point out where Washington, D.C., is on a map, much less Iraq or Afghanistan. Think about that the next time you read a public opinion poll. Yet, at the same time, many feel supremely qualified to make all kinds of remarks on a wide range of subjects. Do you ever read the comments that people write after a news story is posted on the Internet?"

"It is better to know a few things well than to know many things poorly," Thomas replied.

"I have never seen those comments," Marie answered, "but if you have read them once and you know the remarks are foolish and ridiculous, why would you go back and read them again?"

"That is a good point," Richard conceded. "The newspapers are not perfect either. The *Journal* is good on business as well as national and foreign affairs. The *Tribune* is okay for local things, but they have way too much fluff and celebrity news."

Thomas contended it was wise to encourage people to read and comprehend the news as best they can and develop some kind of discernment instead of abandoning them to folly. "I would advise anyone to take the time to read a newspaper carefully and to really think about an issue for some time before taking any side, for or against."

"You are right. We certainly do need a better informed populace, and I understand how easy the distractions can be. I am hoping that during Lent, I will finally and totally control my Internet usage," Richard said. "One minute I would be researching current events, and the next I would be tempted to buy something I really don't need while at the same time getting all caught up with what clothing people wore to the Grammys and the Academy Awards."

"How did those turn out, Rich? I did not see them," Thomas asked.

"Apart from the fashions, I could not tell you. I really can't stomach watching music and movie celebrities pat one another on the back in an attempt to steady their fragile egos. If you ever want to know, though, how important and indispensable modern music and movies are to the world, just ask those show business people. They will tell you in no uncertain terms."

"McGee, I swear, if you are holding anything back," Scott threatened with the desperate calm of a psychopath, pointing a trembling index finger to the ceiling.

"Sorry, Scotty. I've got nothing." The coolness of Richard's reply sent Scott away in a fury.

"Richard, if you don't mind, tell us about the wedding," Marie requested.

"Well, the bride did have the audacity to wear white." Richard's newly acquired level of temperance did not carry over into the level of charity he applied toward his new sister-in-law.

After accepting the inevitability of the situation and the reality that his brother shared some responsibility for it, Richard did his best to make the event as pleasant as possible, mainly by staying as far away as he could from Lisa and her family, whom Richard only referred to as "she" and "they." "They" wanted a massive Westminster Abbey-type royal ceremony, a motorcade to the Conrad Hilton downtown, and a lavish reception in the grand ballroom. But because "they" had no means of paying for all this, their credit cards having already been confiscated along with their foreclosed home, it did not take much for Mr. and Mrs. McGee to insist on and receive a Mass at Queen of Peace Church, followed by a small dinner for family and friends in a neighborhood banquet hall. Instead of putting up resistance, "she" decided she would have a kegger for her "real reception" a few months later.

The day went off as well as could be expected. Chuck was shaky in the morning before Mass and confessed how foolish he had been and how nervous he felt. The enormity of the event seemed to hit him at once, but he faced up to his fears without resorting to alcohol. Margaret

Clarke and a few other parishioners attended the beautiful afternoon Mass. Richard was the best man and, at the dinner, offered a heartfelt wish of happiness for the new couple. In the end, "they" wound up falling down drunk and challenging some members of the wait staff to a fistfight out in the parking lot.

"I did what I could to keep my mouth shut and soldier on through it, for Chuck's sake and for my mom and dad."

"That was a difficult situation to be put in, Richard," Marie said. "Your actions were commendable."

"Thank you." Bitterness remained in his voice. "It was not easy, let me tell you. My sister, Laura, refused to be in the bridal party. If you could have seen the size of those bride's maids, what they were wearing, and the things those grown women did at the reception, you would understand why I got out of there as soon as I could."

"So is it safe to say that neither you nor your sister will be attending the upcoming kegger?" Thomas asked.

"Maybe we will pitch in for the tap. Chuck is on his own for the party, though." Richard let out a sigh. "The whole thing was tough, but I think it will work out. Despite everything, Chuck is a good man. Actually, I was unsure about how he really felt about her until I saw him give her a grade-one kiss at the dinner."

"A grade-one kiss? What is that?" Marie asked.

A pained look momentarily crossed Richard's face. "Captain Virtue never told you about that, huh? The four categories of kisses?"

Marie, becoming more intrigued, shook her head in the negative.

"Well, I suppose I can tell you now." A slight blush filled Richard's cheeks before he continued. "Grade four, the lowest kind, is the one you are forced into in awkward social situations, usually by someone you don't know that well but who wants to pretend like you are a close friend. There is no genuine emotion at all in that kiss. Grade three is one of pure lust, like the kind you see all the time on television and in movies. It's the type of kiss that says 'I am going to use you like a piece of meat, baby, then toss you aside like yesterday's garbage.'"

"It is rather popular," Thomas interjected.

"And rather vulgar," Marie added.

"Grade two is the kiss you give to a relative. There is real love in it, but it is given to your mother or grandmother. You know what I mean. Now, the highest and best kiss, a grade one, is a kiss of pure, true love between a man and a woman."

"Thomas came up with this list?" Marie asked, incredulous at never having heard about it before.

"No, I did not. Richard did. I was made to swear an oath never to reveal it. Richard is the one who mentioned it, not I."

Richard became embarrassed when Marie looked at him and said, "I had no idea you were such a romantic."

"Yeah, well, the list developed over time after I watched *The Princess Bride*," Richard stumbled briefly. "Anyway, there are subtle variations of the grade one. The highest kind is a kiss of pure love from a pure heart. That is the most noble and honorable grade one, and there have only been a few of those in all of human existence. I would not put Chuck's kiss in that high category, but I do believe—no matter how much the thought turns my stomach—that Chuck does love this girl. They can build on that."

Marie was stunned and looked at Thomas as Scott arrived for one last irrational attempt to cling to any lifeline that anyone could throw him.

Richard stood up slowly and looked at Scott, who was now panting like a rabid dog and whose veins were now popping out of his neck and forehead. "Scott, do you really want to know the truth? My dad's work as a state representative is a part-time job. Most state business is taken care of in little chunks of time, usually a week or two, and then they all go on break for a while. When he is in Springfield, he sits on seven or eight committees that deal with the most boring topics you could possibly imagine. And, believe it or not, not every elected official is the sharpest knife in the drawer. When he is not there, he is at his law office or at home. There is no secret information. I can guarantee that he is not sitting around watching all this news like you are. Handle it. January and February are behind us. The Cubs started spring training a few weeks ago, and that means nice weather is right around the corner. We are all going to start getting our college acceptance letters soon, and the world will move on. Get a grip."

"No, you are lying. You are just trying to make me look bad."

"You don't need any of my help for that, Scott. You are doing a great job all by yourself. If you would like, I will tell you what I know from what I have read about it in the newspaper, a credible source of information. You know, if you follow these stories day after day, you get a basic idea about what is going on in the world, but it doesn't make you, me, or anyone else an expert. So if you really want to know my opinion, I will give you my opinion."

Scott looked as if he was about to start frothing at the mouth, and then he suddenly walked away, convinced the nation's financial cataclysm was about to reach its conclusive apex.

"What a pest," Richard said as he turned and saw Susan walk in. He excused himself from Thomas and Marie and went to have a more pleasant conversation with her.

CHAPTER 21

The new streetlight at North Shore Avenue and Sheridan Road could now display how many seconds there were until the green light turned yellow and then to red. A digital zero and six suddenly popped up for the traffic headed eastbound on North Shore, forcing pedestrians and drivers to decide immediately whether to speed up and try to beat the red light or to stop and wait.

Walking past stately and familiar three-flat apartment buildings, Margaret Clarke approached the corner as a cold drizzle began to fall from the overcast April sky. Flatts and Sharpe Music Company was just across the street. The temperature was in the low forties, but with the blustery wind, the rain felt like sharp, little ice pellets. The unpleasant thought of standing and waiting while getting soaked to the bone made Margaret quickly decide to scurry across Sheridan Road, though she did so only after scanning all around for any of the crazed hotrod maniacs who somehow managed to appear in these instances out of nowhere at the last second.

An old-fashioned bell rang as she opened the door to the venerable and charming neighborhood music store, and once inside, she shook the rain from her jacket. A head popped out of the office in the back of the store to whom Margaret addressed an apology, "Sorry about the mess, Chris."

"Don't worry about it," the new owner replied as she came out to greet one of her regular customers. "It looks nasty out there."

"It is, but the clouds are breaking up, and the sun looks like it wants to come out sooner or later. I don't mind a day or two like this. You know it is not going to last. It is supposed to be warm and sunny for Easter Sunday."

"Let's hope so," Chris stated doubtfully. A spring weather forecast for Chicago could change dramatically by the hour. "Is there anything I can help you with today, Margaret?"

"No, thank you. I just need blank manuscript paper and some sheet music."

"Okay, you know where they are at. Let me know when you are ready to check out."

Margaret came around the register and display case, which also doubled as the instrument repair area, and made her way into the room filled with music books, trying to decide what would be the best song with a spring theme for her students to learn. Vivaldi, Strauss, Wagner, and Tchaikovsky were all good candidates, but for some reason, Mendelssohn's *Spring Song* seemed to fit best. Certainly well known, Margaret had heard it for the first time as a child in a cartoon. It was a beautiful piece with a whimsical nature that seemed to induce a childlike release from the troubles of life. Surrendering to the happiness provided by something that was simply beautiful seemed particularly appropriate this Easter season.

While ringing up the sale, Chris mentioned that she was thinking about adding some rooms in the back of the store to expand the number of lessons offered and that she might need a few more instructors in the summer. Margaret could not commit to anything now, but it was an intriguing and generous offer. They would definitely talk more about it in the future. Margaret said good-bye as the rain began to lighten up.

The bell on the door rang again as Margaret turned south on Sheridan. The light turned yellow, and she began to rush across the street but then hesitated, briefly catching sight of a familiar face quickly coming toward her. The approaching woman was hunched over, lips tightly pursed, with white earbuds firmly in place, an obscuring hood draped over her head, and a polyester bag clutched with both hands. Margaret stopped to try and recognize this person who bore such a sad and sour look. The woman's gaze never left the sidewalk ten feet in front of her as she tried to brush past Margaret, who might as well have been a signpost. The woman was terribly startled and looked around in horror when Margaret lightly tapped her shoulder and asked, "Anne, is that you?"

Ten minutes earlier, Anne Martin had finished working out at the St. Aloysius University Recreational Center and was loading up her workout bag for the short walk home. As an alumna of the nursing school, it was convenient and cheaper for her to join the university rec center than to join a health club, not that it really mattered where she worked out. Her poor eating and sleeping habits negated much of the benefits of her physical activity. The exercise, for now, only made her more exhausted.

At least she realized that something needed to be done. Things could not continue on the way they had been going. Fifteen minutes on a stationary bicycle, ten minutes on a treadmill, and a few sets on the machines was all she could manage after a three-year break. The dismal output only added to her sense of hopelessness and anger at the world, and she often sat with a million discouraging thoughts whirling around in her mind.

A towel, an iPod, and her purse were harshly thrown into the polyester bag, and she grabbed her jacket and forced herself into it as if the jacket was resisting her somehow. The earbuds were set in place, the music turned up, and her hood pulled over her head. Her forearm muscles clenched the bag tightly as she stood up, slammed into the exit door shoulder first, and was met with a gust of freezing rain in her face. *When will this God-forsaken winter end?* she thought. The five-block walk home seemed like fifty miles.

The students were on spring break, and Anne quickly made her way past the old gymnasium and through the empty campus. Turning north on Sheridan Road, she saw a few young girls waiting to cross the street and thought of Marie. That caused her to pause briefly and watch the girls go into the elevated train station and head downtown. Even that seemed depressing to her. A quick surge of rain and cold whipped her face, which tightened in anger, along with her neck, back, and shoulders.

Trudging along, she noticed the advertisements on the walls of businesses and on the shelter of the bus stop. One was of an overly confident young man wearing the latest in fashionable clothing. Another proclaimed the miracles and wonders of mobile communication. She could not tell exactly what another was trying to sell; it only seemed to entice young ladies with the benefits of drinking vodka, dressing as provocatively as possible, and throwing themselves at the first stranger who catches their eye.

There was nothing new in any of them. Anne Martin had seen similar advertisements for most of her adult life, but now they also seemed depressing. This unbridled materialism was the gift her generation had given to her daughter's generation. That brought new thoughts of resentment and self-loathing: *What will happen to Marie? College is so expensive, and there are no jobs for graduates now anyway. What's the point? And just look at this neighborhood. There was a double homicide one mile from here last week. I have to get Marie away from this dump. But where do we go? How did everything get so messed up all of a sudden? What am I supposed to do now? What am I going to do when Marie is gone?*

The sudden hand on her shoulder frightened Anne

Martin beyond belief, and she recoiled. She vaguely recognized the voice calling to her, and she pulled her hood back to see a familiar face with a gentle smile. "Oh my God! Margaret?" Anne said, panting to catch her breath. "You scared the hell out of me."

"I am sorry, Anne. It's nice to see you, though. It's been a long time. How are you?"

"Oh, I'm fine, considering how oppressive this weather is. It is absolutely frigid out today. This winter will never end. I mean, my God! And how are you?" The question was asked without any hint of real concern.

"I am doing well. Thank you. You know—"

"I've heard that your Thomas is at West Ridge now." It came across almost like an accusation.

"Yes, he—"

"Did you hear about all the alcohol and drugs that are running rampant at that school? I don't know why the mayor and the police don't do something about it. What the hell is wrong with them? Some kid is going to die there soon enough. Don't send your young one there unless you want her to be some kind of wino or druggie."

Long ago, Anne Martin fell into the vice of talking at people instead of conversing with them, continuously issuing bold, definitive statements that in her mind gave the final say on any topic. And, in doing so, she became one of those curious modern creatures who never talk to other people in any substantial way. Their statements leave no place for continued discussion, and those who do not speak in this manner find such individuals to be unpleasant company. But more strangely, even those people who use this modern type of Internet-forum, lecture-giving speech don't like to be around others who speak in the same manner. So they isolate themselves away from society and never end up talking to anyone ever.

Margaret tried to start a new subject. "So you and Marie are back at St. Aloysius Parish? You are very fortunate. That church is beautiful. It is so nice that they have been able to keep it up."

"And you are at Queen of Heaven? I am sure you know about the troubles they are having there. God only knows how long that school will stay open. The archdiocese should look into their finances and the way that pastor lives it up. It's a disgrace," Anne said, shaking her head. There was always a nervousness in the way she spoke, and the boldness seemed like an attempt to cover up a tremendous lack of confidence.

Anne began to ask if there was any news about the ovarian cyst the young Lydon girl had developed recently, but Margaret cut her off and asked directly, "Anne, it has been over three years since Jim and your mother died, and I am certain they have been very hard years. How are you really?"

The question caused Anne to stop mid-sentence and look at Margaret with eyes displaying a thousand emotions churning all at once. Anne stepped back and put her hand up to her mouth. There was a short pause before she replied sharply, "It has been hard, trying to do everything myself." Staring even more intently at Margaret she went on, her emotions getting the better of her, "I don't know. How can you understand? You have never lost anyone close to you." After a brief moment, Anne's face turned white, and her eyes welled up with tears. "Oh, Margaret! I am so sorry. I was not thinking." Her defenses completely fell away, and her body seemed to shrink back. "Please forgive me."

Many years ago, Anne Martin was at Indian Boundary Park when Margaret's nineteen-year-old brother, Robert, crossed the street on his bicycle and was hit and killed by a drunk driver in broad daylight. Watching Margaret hold her younger brother's hand as he died on the curb was the saddest thing Anne had ever personally witnessed in her life. She also knew full well that Margaret had suffered two miscarriages between Thomas and Kathleen.

As Anne fell into uncontrollable sobbing, Margaret put

her arm around her and looked for somewhere to go. There was a small Starbucks wedged in the corner of the New 400 Movie Theater building, but the traffic light quickly began its six-second countdown. Margaret waited patiently, helping Anne to pull herself together, and then took her across the street where they could talk.

The lovely outdoor patio would have been ideal in nicer weather, but they settled for a small table inside by the door as Margaret went up to order. When Margaret came back, Anne was calmer, but she looked incredibly drained and feeble as Margaret set down her coffee.

After taking a sip that seemed to rejuvenate her some, Anne spoke meekly, "You know, when I was a kid, my mother tried to teach me all these things about how to be a respectable lady: manners, speech, consideration. When I was a kid, I did what she asked. But as soon as my teenage years came, I did not want anything to do with any of it. I went along with the crowd, and we were so sure of ourselves. Sex, drugs, rock and roll, the do-whatever-you-want-just-to-have-fun mentality. That is what it was all about. Then when we got a little older, at the age when my mother had been married with two kids already, I met Jim, and we just kept on doing the same thing. My parents were very disappointed. I know they did not like Jim, but what could they do? My father died when I was seventeen, and my mother could not control me. Jim and I eventually got married and had Marie, but it really never stopped—the mindset, I mean. Look at what it has given me now." Her eyes drifted off.

"Anne, we all made mistakes growing up."

"That is just it. My mother was right all along. I would not have made those mistakes if I had followed what she said, but I would not listen. I was too full of myself, and those twenty-five years of fun have only brought me misery. My mother knew better. Now she's gone, and I can never tell her that."

Margaret reassured her friend, "I don't know anyone

our age who looks back on her youth and wishes she had drunk more alcohol or done more of any other foolish thing. Leave those bad things where they are: in the past. You do have one very good thing—here and now—that came out of your marriage. Marie is an absolutely wonderful girl."

"I thank God she never followed my example. What should a young girl do as she grows up, except to follow what her mother did as far as being a wife and a mother? I was given a beautiful example that had been passed on for centuries, and I spit on it and threw it aside. What example did I give Marie besides a disgraceful one? I can't even remember a sliver of the things my mother taught me. How can I pass them on to my daughter now? All those little things that were so important are gone forever." Anne's self-loathing showed on her face. "I have forgotten everything my mother taught me, but at least Marie had her grandmother around for a short time. They were very close, like kindred spirits. Whatever grace and refinement Marie has came from her grandmother . . . and, I suppose, from you." Anne paused, then looked down. "I never thanked you for that because I resented it. Your family seemed so perfect, and mine was not. I know our problems were not your fault. It just felt sometimes, though, like Marie wanted to be at the Clarke house more than the Martin house. I can't blame her really. What happened to Jim that night could have happened any one of ten dozen times over the past twenty years."

Margaret took Anne's hand and said tenderly, "Anne, Marie loves you more than anyone in the world, and she knows you love her."

"I know she loves me, and I have treated her horribly. She has never once had a thought in her head that would ever cause her to blush before anyone, and I resented her because of that. After those two died, looking at Marie was like looking at my mother, and all I could feel was how much I had let both my daughter and my mother down.

Marie was everything that I was not because she had chosen the right path, and I had not. And yet, Marie never stopped loving me. What did I ever do to have a child like that? I feel like a complete failure as a parent."

"Every parent who has ever lived has felt the same way at one time or another. You still have time to set things right." Anne was inconsolable, and Margaret asked her, "What are you and Marie doing for Easter?"

"Nothing special. My brother is going to his in-laws, so I was going to have a small dinner for the two of us before I have to go to work."

"Why don't you come over for dinner with us?"

"I would not feel right doing that."

"You are most welcome in our house anytime, and I think Marie would enjoy it as well."

After thinking about it for a few moments, Anne replied, "You are probably right. Thank you." She sat quietly, thinking about all the petty gossip she had tried to spread about the Clarke family over the years. Margaret knew about it but never said a word. Anne looked up suddenly and inquired, "Why have you been so kind to me and my family?"

"When we were in grammar school at St. Titus, the nuns would always respond to that question with a saying that I never fully understood until I became much older. Do you remember it?"

"No. What was that?"

"We are all Cretans."

CHAPTER 22

With spring break over and less than two months until the end of the school year, Ms. Sullivan was expecting a struggle to keep her students attentive to their studies. Even she could not help but dream of summer vacation from time to time. Most of the AP/Honors students, however, were locked in on the scarce time remaining in school for determining the final class rankings and deciding the class valedictorian. The competition was getting fierce.

Despite her best efforts, these students were wound up tight, but she was not going to let herself get caught up in that. Becoming the faculty moderator of the Debate Club seemed like a welcome diversion from the tension of the classroom, and it also could be a useful way for the students to relax and release some of their stress.

The interscholastic debates had strict and formal rules on how they were conducted. With a week before the first competition, though, Ms. Sullivan wanted her debaters in today's practice session to informally discuss a topic and develop their ability to think rationally, off the top of their head. Not having cue cards and prepared research papers at their disposal caused a disconcerted murmuring from most in the room.

She almost threw up her hand in disgust, trying to convince the fearful that they would not be dismissed from the team for a less-than-stellar showing today. She would even let the students decide what topic to discuss. That set off a mad rush for their cell phones to search for a subject to discuss and to find some ammunition to use on one side or the other. This activity was squelched immediately, as Ms. Sullivan forced them to turn off their phones. She then went around and collected them all, placing them on her desk. The room was somber.

"Come on, somebody. Give me a topic being discussed in the news today." For the young teacher, it was like trying to pull a crooked nail out of a piece of wood without a hammer. "It can be on any subject: local, international, political, educational, scientific. Anything."

"How about the federal government's funding of state and local infrastructure projects?"

"Nice try, Mr. Connelly, but no." That was the topic for the first competition next week.

"Come on. Anything other than that," she pleaded.

She looked around at the squirming group and was about to suggest a topic when Scott Weber blurted out, "Gays in the military." It was a more controversial subject than she wanted, but a student came up with it, and this was only a practice exercise.

"Okay, Mr. Weber. Would you like to take the position for or against allowing homosexuals to serve openly in the military?"

"For."

"Will anyone take the side against? Mr. Clarke, all right."

All fifteen students were seated around a table, with the opponents facing each other. Scott would begin, and Thomas would follow. They would control the discussion, while Ms. Sullivan would observe and intervene only as necessary. Scott was given a few moments to think about and organize his opening statement before beginning.

"The United States of America is based on freedom and equality. For too long, certain members of the military, and of the population as a whole, have been oppressed and forced to hide who they are by unfair, hateful, and bigoted rules that prevent them from serving openly. Gay men and women have proudly served in the military for years. It is now time for our country to move forward from prejudice and an old-fashioned mindset. We must think more openly and inclusively about people's sexual orientation and accept them for who they are. We must have justice and equality for all."

Thomas replied, "The military can only be effective when order and discipline are adhered to rigorously. Order is preferable to disorder, especially in the military, because without it, people in an already dangerous and deadly situation are unnecessarily placed in even more risk. The safety of the country is then put in jeopardy. An infantry unit, an air wing, and a naval ship cannot function properly without order and discipline. The needs of the unit must take precedence over the wishes of the individual.

"This hierarchical structure in the military reflects a natural order where those of greater authority issue orders to those of lesser authority. Each member of this military hierarchy, though, is imperfect and finite. There are no perfect orders. All are issued by an imperfect superior to an imperfect subordinate. There are no perfect laws that originate from any imperfect man. The imperfect by nature can only generate the imperfect.

"The perfect and infinite are preferable to the imperfect and finite. Wisdom is preferable to foolishness. A wise man recognizes his imperfection and chooses what is unchanging; eternal; and perfectly true, just, and good for all so that all can live truly free. Individuals must sacrifice for the common good. But before we continue, I think we should establish a basic understanding of certain words and terms. Scott, how would you define freedom?"

"Freedom means that people can choose to live as they wish to live, and no one can impose their views on anyone else. Individuals can do as they please and love whomever they wish to love. And these decisions must be accepted by all."

"What you described is not freedom. It is freedom's opposite: licentiousness. In the natural order, a higher authority will grant a license, or a permission, to someone or something of a lower order to perform a certain activity. For example, one must have a driver's license issued by the state to operate a motor vehicle. Many businesses require a city or state business license to operate. There are rules and limitations imposed on those who apply for these licenses. People must drive safely and under control of their faculties, for instance. Businesses must operate lawfully and justly. Civil order depends on these limitations.

"Licentiousness, which springs from pride, is the vice that destroys civil order, military order, and a well-ordered soul. A licentious individual chooses to do whatever he or she feels. A weak, imperfect human being has a natural tendency toward vice and sin and becomes controlled—and eventually enslaved—by passions, emotions, and sensual desires.

"Homosexuals wish to give themselves a license to set their own moral limits or to not set any at all. They are asking for society to accept as natural and good this disordered enslavement. It is disordered because their sensual desires, which are disordered in and of themselves, have upended reason and love in the command of their soul. If licentiousness is granted for homosexuals and enshrined in law, then it must be granted and enshrined in law for all. What is true for one man is true for all men. As a consequence, everyone in the military and in society as a whole can then do whatever they wish, without any individual or any government telling them their actions are wrong. This is foolishness. Wisdom is preferable to foolishness. Virtue is preferable to vice. Freedom is preferable to slavery. Order is preferable to disorder. The unchanging, perfect, and eternal are preferable to the mutable, imperfect, and finite."

"You are just a cruel, hateful, bigot trying to force other people to think like you do," Scott said in a huff.

Thomas responded calmly, "Argumentum ad hominem and argumentum ad misericordiam."

Ms. Sullivan stepped in. "Mr. Weber, you cannot take these arguments personally. This is a debate, not a cable news show or an Internet blog. You must be respectful to your opponent." Scott was still worked up, so she turned to Thomas and said, "Mr. Clarke, please explain what those Latin words mean and give your definition of freedom. You failed to do that in your response."

"You are right. I am sorry, Ms. Sullivan. The words in Latin were names of two common logical fallacies, which exhibit deficiencies in logic. When Scott defined freedom, his statement could only be true or deficient in truth. If I could not show a deficiency in his definition, then I must accept his definition as true. My response attempted to show, using reason and logic, where his argument was lacking or false. By the same reasoning, my response could only be true or deficient in truth. What Scott said in reply to it was a personal attack on me—ad hominem—and an appeal to pity—ad misericordiam. He did not attempt to use reason or logic to refute my statement."

"Mr. Weber, do you understand that? Your debating position loses credibility when you resort to those tactics. It is better to concede and move on if you don't have logical refutation."

"Yes, ma'am." Scott was still upset.

Ms. Sullivan signaled for Thomas to continue. "I would define freedom as not only the ability to do what is good, true, and just but also the need to take responsibility for one's actions. True freedom comes from the perfection of virtue. In this country, we are not forced by the government to spy on one another or to bear false witness and commit acts of perjury against our neighbors as has happened in former communist states as well as to those currently living under a despot. Also, no one is forced by law into a state of servile bondage. Free men do not suffer these external oppressions nor do they impose on themselves an internal slavery in their soul to passions, emotions, and sensual desires. Eternal truth and love command their soul. The well-ordered soul commands the mind, and the mind controls the bodily activities. Again, order is preferable to disorder, the eternal to the finite. I believe when one considers various older writings, including those of the Founding Fathers, in light of this classical understanding of freedom, one gains a deeper and fuller understanding of the principles of which they wrote and that they strived to adhere to."

Scott sat stewing over an answer for a few moments before Ms. Sullivan goaded him for a response. He had nothing but chose to press on along another path. "How can this country call itself just when it forces some citizens to live in a second-class status and denies them the rights that all other citizens enjoy? Why must people who don't comply with the norm be called out as different and constantly be misunderstood? Is everything in black and white? Are there no gray areas? If someone thinks differently than you, how does that affect anyone else? Justice and civil rights must be given to all, or else this nation is only a hypocritical joke."

"Scott, how do you define justice?"

"Oh, come on!" Scott replied angrily. "He's trying to play with words to trip me up."

"I assure you, Ms. Sullivan, that is not my intention," Thomas replied ever temperately. He then held up a pencil. "If I call this an elephant, and you call it a pencil, we cannot have a rational discussion about this object."

"That is fair enough, Mr. Clarke. Mr. Weber, please give your definition of justice and also keep in mind that this is only a classroom exercise."

"Fine," Scott said harshly. He thought for a second and then stated firmly, "Justice would be when everyone is treated the same and when laws are in place that ensure this. No one can say another person's life is wrong, sinful, or immoral. You can't make people deny who they are and the way they were born. Everybody must be treated the same, even if you don't agree with them or how they live. Women have rights over their own bodies. Gays have rights. Everyone has rights."

"I would agree that a component of justice is giving your fellow man what he is due. But, in the order of those who should be given their due, then God should be given His due first and foremost. Yet again, order is preferable to disorder. God is of the highest nature—far above the nature of man—and is the source and summit of Truth and Goodness. God must get His due as well.

"Imperfect men can only write imperfect laws. Because an imperfect law is written in a book somewhere does not make it just. Only the perfect can generate the perfect. The laws of God are unchanging, perfect, and eternal because God is their source. A good and wise man seeks the immutable, not the mutable. The perfect, not the imperfect. The eternal, not the finite. To watch an imperfect, prideful man show distain when he is chastised for his actions is like, as Dumas wrote, watching an ant on a blade of grass raise his fists and shake them in self-righteous indignation at the all-powerful God and His precepts.

"Plato writes that doing what is unjust is more to be guarded against than suffering it. Man was created to serve and love God, first and foremost, and then to serve and love his neighbor out of that love for God. The man who loves himself first loves imperfectly and in a disordered manner. One must assume responsibility for an action taken of free will."

Scott replied quickly, "How can anyone say that when two people love each other, it is wrong? Our society should be encouraging all loving couples, even if they are different from some antiquated norm. Love is love. There is no difference. We need more support of loving couples in this country and less homophobia and hatred."

"How would you define love?"

"Oh please! You want me to define love?"

"How can you say two people are in love if you can't define what that is?"

"Oh my God!" Scott said, throwing his head back, putting his hand over his eyes in frustration, and scowling. "Love is whatever I want it to be," he declared. Ms. Sullivan reminded him again that this was an exercise, and she gently pushed him to try his best.

"All right. Love is when two people have feelings for each other and understand each other," he blurted out, embarrassed. "Certain people have a kind of chemistry between them. They enjoy each other's company and like doing things together. I don't know."

Thomas responded, "Love is an act of the will, not only an emotion. There are times when the people you love do certain things and you do not feel like loving them at that moment. It is a pure act of the will to force yourself to continue to love a particular person even when you are infuriated with him or her.

"Love is unitive, joining two souls into one. It is self-sacrificing, and it is also life giving. Love desires, for the sake of the beloved, that which is of the greatest and highest nature in existence. God is of the greatest and highest nature: unchanging, perfect, and eternal. Therefore, if you truly love someone, you seek for your beloved to have perfect and eternal union with God. A husband who loves his wife and a wife who loves her husband each does whatever is necessary to get their spouse into heaven. There is nothing higher to be sought. But a heart is only made pure to love as it should by obedience to Truth. One cannot say 'I love you' to another and then turn around and ask that person to do anything that would separate him or her from God."

Scott was incensed and said, "People can love anyone in any way they want to without resorting to cruel, ridiculous, hateful bigotry."

Thomas countered quickly. "If a mother sees her child about to drink poison and slaps the poison from the child's hands, that is a loving act, not a hateful one. If you saw someone pick up a hatchet and attempt to mutilate their arm and you forcibly stopped them, that would also be a loving act. Now, if you saw someone about to commit an act of violence against their own soul—to mutilate or even murder the very essence of their being—and you did not try to stop them but rather encouraged and enticed them to continue, that would be a most hateful and evil act. The first two spiritual acts of *mercy* are to admonish the sinner and to instruct the ignorant. A good and wise individual strives to love rather than hate, and that wise person also strives to love in a perfect and heavenly way rather than an imperfect and human way."

"The 'imperfect man,' as you insist on calling everyone, cannot love perfectly," Scott retorted angrily. "No one has ever loved like that ever, and there are no religious people today who love like that."

"Man is weak and imperfect because of his sins, but has been made in the image and likeness of God, especially regarding the soul's capacity to recognize Truth and to love. Jesus Christ on the Cross gave a perfect example of this love: unitive, self-sacrificing, life-giving, and desiring the greatest and highest for the sake of the beloved. That sacrifice gave us the gift of sanctifying grace so that we can love in a perfect, heavenly manner."

Scott was seething with fury as Thomas continued, "If you are going to examine a teaching, philosophy, or religion, you can't look at its worst examples. Rather, you must consider the best examples. Look at the people who live up to the exact letter of that teaching or religion and then see if it is better or worse than whatever path you are following now. I would put up the teachings and life of Jesus Christ and the holy saints for anyone to examine."

"Nobody has to accept what you say. People can believe whatever they want to."

"I agree. Each of us has a free will. It is up to the listener to hear both sides and then decide for himself or herself the higher and better course of action. It also follows that if one rejects the higher course of action in an act of free will, one must accept as well the consequences of that decision without complaint."

"Okay, you have both strayed off topic a little bit," Ms. Sullivan interjected, "but that was a good discussion. Mr. Weber, you resorted to a few more logical fallacies in your responses, but we can go over them before the first competition. I would like you both to give a final statement, and stay on topic, please. Mr. Weber, you first."

Through clenched teeth, Scott reiterated his stance for equality, justice, and freedom for all. No one should be told that how they live and how they love is immoral or wrong. According to Scott, we must move past this outdated mentality of fear and hate to a more progressive and modern one of inclusion and acceptance.

Thomas replied, "Virtue exalts a nation, but sin is a people's disgrace. A man is only as great as he appears in the eyes of God and no more. If one feels the painful sting of a charitable and proper chastisement, that pain suffered is not unjust nor is it the result of hatred and fear. Only fools despise wisdom and instruction. Milton would say that none can love freedom heartily but good men; the rest love not freedom but license. One cannot simply say, 'Left is right. Up is down. Evil is good. Truth is falsehood.' Good men speak and live the truth in and out of season. Order is preferred to disorder. It is the perfection of virtue that leads to true freedom, peace, happiness, and love."

CHAPTER 23

Sitting alone in the lunchroom, Thomas had a rare moment to think. Even though he was in a room filled with other students, his table was empty and his mind was clear, unaffected by the massive spring storm that was rolling through the city. Powerful claps of thunder shook the entire building to its core. The interior lights flickered momentarily after a nearby lightning strike, and the howling winds caused the school's structure to sway and creak. These storms were a regular occurrence in May, but for those who had never experienced a Midwestern land-based hurricane, they could be terrifying.

Thomas sat with various letters of acceptance before him, ranging from Stanford to Brown to Fordham, among others. A decision had to be made soon. The decision was complicated by the fact that the deal to sell the family print shop building had fallen through. His family certainly could have used the extra the money it would have provided, but his father was probably more relieved than upset. The drop in business had leveled off; the company could survive. Things would be tight, though, until the economy picked up again. John Clarke had decided to partition off the back of the building and rent it out as office space, though there was a glut of office space for rent elsewhere and very few prospective tenants.

Thomas let those problems go for the moment and returned to a book on chivalry by Geoffroi de Charny, a fourteenth-century man-at-arms. He was struck by the urging of this famous knight to his brethren not to seek fine clothing, a soft bed, long hours of sleep, and a sumptuous meal with only the right foods but rather to constantly prepare themselves for the rigors and hardships of combat. Even more so, Thomas was impressed with the teaching that an honorable knight should love honorably. Nothing in his conduct should ever bring dishonor or shame to the woman he loves. He should also never cause his beloved to commit any disgraceful act. A good knight, above all, should always defend the honor of his beloved. Thomas could use that in the future, so he decided to lock it away in the vault of his memory.

Richard came up to the table and sat across from Thomas, looking as if he had news hot off the presses. "You have been holding out on me again," he began.

"How so?"

"You did not tell me that you let Scotty Fantastic have it in a debate."

"That was weeks ago, and it was only an exercise for the Debate Club."

"Well, Ms. Sullivan was mighty impressed and wrote a glowing report about it to Dr. Diaz. For a guy who isn't even gay, Scott sure was a passionate defender of the cause. They do have a relentless PR machine in the media, though. He certainly bought what they are selling."

"A debate is not a personal argument between two people. Scott's uncontrolled passions in that practice debate was his main downfall. He did a good job in the actual competition."

"That's great," Richard replied with condescension. "Boy, I wish I could have seen you let him have it. What do you have here?" He pointed to the letters.

"I have to make a choice in the next two days, and then I have to think about how much it will cost and how to pay for it all."

"If it makes any difference, I am going to St. Aloysius."

"Really? Wasn't your dad pushing for the University of Chicago?"

"He was, and I did get accepted, but I think he had something to do with that. I had no choice about where I went to high school, so I want to have a choice about where I go to college. It took a little while, but he eventually gave in, especially when I told him I was thinking about pre-law and eventually getting a JD. It's his alma mater."

"Congratulations."

"Thanks. The other news I wanted to tell you—"

Richard was suddenly interrupted by Susan and Marie, both of whom appeared mildly upset. They apologized, and when pressed for the cause of their agitation, they reluctantly related how Rex Burger made unwanted, crude advances toward both girls. When he was rebuffed in no uncertain terms, Rex responded in vulgar and savage words shouted down the hallway.

Thomas listened to the tale, and his calm demeanor did not change, but Marie noticed a flicker in his eyes that she had never seen before, and it sent a shudder down her spine. An infuriated Richard began to spew venom as Thomas calmly stood up, grabbed his bag, and walked away from the table without saying a word.

Marie yelled out desperately, "Richard, Richard, stop him!"

Before Richard or Susan could figure out what had happened, Thomas was leaving the cafeteria, and the three gave chase.

Rex was slowly strolling down the hallway, regaling a small group of followers with a story of one of his latest adventures. "So I'm in my dad's Buick, and I come up to a stop sign. After I stop, this guy in a BMW comes up to the cross street on my left. And then guess what? He tries to wave me through, like I'm his boy or something. Nobody gives me the wave through. I give the wave through to other people. So I sat there for like ten minutes and wouldn't budge."

A blur came up next to Rex and forcefully shoved him into the lockers. After letting out a womanly screech, Rex looked around and whimpered. "What hell is your problem, Clarke? Get away from me!" Thomas put his right hand on Rex's right shoulder and pinned his forearm into Rex's neck. Even though Rex had gained a least thirty pounds from the end of the football season, Thomas lifted him off his feet.

Richard came running up, scanning the hallway for faculty or security. The coast was clear, but he told Thomas to hurry. Richard turned his back on the two and nervously kept watch. Thomas quickly glanced back at the gathering crowd as Marie and Susan arrived. He got up close to Rex, pointed with his free hand toward the two aggrieved young ladies, and whispered something quietly. Rex meekly nodded, and Thomas let him fall to the ground in a blubbering mass. Somewhere, somehow, at that moment, Pierre Terrail, Chevalier de Bayard, was proud and happy to know that chivalry was not dead and that there was at least one good man left in the world without fear and beyond reproach to defend the honor of a daughter of France. Thomas caught Marie's eye as she gently smiled.

Richard tried his best to disperse the crowd when William approached. He shook his head ever so slightly at the pitiable sight of Rex, then came up to Thomas and informed him that Dr. Diaz would like to see him.

"That's the other news I had for you," Richard said. Thomas, still exhibiting an impressive display of temperance, asked Richard to take the girls back to the cafeteria, and he left for the principal's office.

Ricardo Diaz put down his phone and began pacing the

room frantically. The mayor would name his new superintendent before the end of the school year, and Dr. Diaz wanted that position badly. Most of his friends and contemporaries were moving up in government and in private industry, and he did not want to be stuck here with all these headaches. A year or two as superintendent of schools would put him in the driver's seat for a very lucrative future.

The Chicago Public Schools Debate Championship was at the end of the week, and if West Ridge could defeat Dunning High, the promotion was his. He needed his best team to put its best foot forward. There was a rustling in the outer office, and Charlene called in to let the principal know who had arrived. Thomas entered and sat in his familiar spot.

"Mr. Clarke, how are you? It has been a long time."

Thomas, who had not been summoned for several weeks, replied, "I am fine, sir. Thank you."

Dr. Diaz reminded Thomas of the upcoming championship and asked how the team was preparing and if everyone was ready.

"I believe we are well prepared. We have all worked very hard, and Ms. Sullivan has come up with a very good strategy. We are ready."

"Are you ready to go personally, Mr. Clarke?"

"I will not be participating personally, sir. I am helping with the team's preparation as best I can, though."

"What do you mean? You have to participate! You have to be up there!" Dr. Diaz was drenched in perspiration and was utterly exasperated. He had gained a lot of weight and lost a lot of hair since their last meeting.

The principal of Dunning had arranged for the topic of the debate to be on whether the state government should withhold funding from private agencies that do not comply with certain state standards. These agencies included those that refuse to provide contraceptives and abortions or facilitate adoptions to gay couples. West

Ridge would be arguing that the state would be right to withhold the funding. Thomas and a few others declined to participate on moral grounds. Ms. Sullivan had no problem with that.

Ricardo Diaz exploded and screamed out loudly that if Thomas did not participate, he could forget about being valedictorian. More importantly, Dr. Diaz vowed to make it his personal mission in life to call every top-tier school that Thomas applied to and ensure he had no chance of getting into any of them ever.

Thomas calmly looked at Dr. Diaz, then at his bag full of acceptance letters. He stood up and cheerfully walked out of the room. The enraged principal made a move toward him, but the door opened, and there was a room full of waiting students who had heard the entire conversation. They were all in shock. Dr. Diaz slammed the door behind Thomas and continued ranting and raving alone in his office.

"Mr. Clarke? Thomas?" Charlene Wilson put her hand on his arm to stop him. She was embarrassed and apologetic. "What Dr. Diaz just said and did is wrong. The way he has treated you all year has been wrong. I am sorry I did not say anything." She looked at the ground.

"Ms. Wilson, it has been an absolute pleasure to know you and to talk with you this past year." He shook her hand and gave her a genuine smile of thanks.

That made her feel worse, and she struggled to find the right words in front of the other students. She pulled him aside and said quietly, "Thank you, Thomas. You have always been most gracious. I just want you to know that a lot of people at the school here agree with the things you have said in your schoolwork, in your papers, and in your speeches. We could never publicly admit that because we could honestly lose our jobs if we did. I wanted you to know that you are not alone. There are people here who are glad you spoke up and said what you did. If you hadn't said it, nobody would have. Thank you."

Thomas thanked her again for the kind words and then went back to the grind. *Three more weeks to go, and then all this will be over*, he reminded himself.

CHAPTER 24

The West Ridge Preparatory Academy graduation ceremony was held in the football stadium under a beautiful, soaring, sunny, and deep blue June sky. The cloudless heavens stretched from horizon to horizon, allowing the event to be moved from the auditorium and its malfunctioning air-conditioning system, and the day went off without a hiccup.

After the ceremony, Thomas was making his way, graduation cap in hand, through the lingering crowd of proud, picture-taking families when Steve Souter came up and shook his hand.

"Congratulations, Thomas."

"Thanks, Steve. And to you as well. How is everything going?"

"Pretty good. I don't really have any money for school, so I am going to join the Air Force for a few years to save up. My dad was in the Army, and he said if he ever had to do it again, he would join the Air Force."

"That's fantastic, Steve. Good luck. What's Rex up to?"

"Well, maybe you haven't heard yet, but Monique is pregnant."

"Oh boy! No, I hadn't heard about that."

"Yeah, anyway, Rex and I really don't hang out anymore. Look, I know you want to get back to your family. I just wanted to thank you. You were always cool to me. I appreciate it."

Thomas shook his hand again. "It was nothing, Steve. I am sure I will see you around. Enjoy the summer as much as you can before boot camp."

Mr. and Mrs. Burger came by without Rex. They were talking with some other parents. Mrs. Burger, wearing her best purple-and-yellow floral print muumuu, assured everyone that they were doing fine. It was hard, though, to give up the finer things in life, such as eating out every day and going on fantastic vacations. It was all the bank's fault anyway. As soon as their lawsuit was settled, the Burgers would be back to their accustomed lifestyle in no time. Mr. Burger proudly bragged of his son's virility in fathering a child.

On the other side of the stadium, State Representative Charles McGee had a large crowd around him. This was the case wherever he went. No matter how many hands were thrust his way, though, he grabbed each one firmly and looked each person in the eye as he said hello. Moving slowly yet steadily, he had to twist and turn to get to everyone, and he accidentally backed into someone. Charles spun around quickly to apologize.

John Clarke beat him to it and said, "Hey, Chuck. I'm sorry. I did not see you. How are you?"

The weary politician gave a signal to his people that he needed a minute, and they moved in to seal off the pressing flesh. It was a much-needed break to simply be Chuck McGee for a short while.

"I'm good, John. How the hell are you? Your leg is all healed up I hope? Say, do you have any water? I'm dying of thirst."

"I am doing fine. It's a great day. I am sure you and Joan are very proud," John replied as he gave his old friend a plastic water bottle. "Isn't it a little strange, though, to have the principal get fired right at the end of the school year?"

After quickly downing the water, Chuck McGee said definitively, "Sometimes a guy can get a little too big for his britches, John. People like that overreach and step on toes they shouldn't step on. I am sure he'll find a job somewhere." Ricardo Diaz received a harsh lesson in raw power, not that Chuck McGee would ever admit to having had any part in it.

"Listen, John, I want to talk to you about something real quick. My state rep's office and my law firm are both required to keep documents for a certain period of time. I hear there is some storage space available in the back of your print shop. If you have not rented it out already, I'd be interested."

John knew these matters were normally taken care of by one of Representative McGee's lower-level people, and he appreciated the graciousness of the offer. "Thanks, Chuck. We could use the rent."

With the wave of a hand, the simple answer came, "Hey, you're helping me out of a spot." Chuck eyed Thomas walking over to Richard and remarked, "You've got a hell of a kid there, John."

The reply came immediately. "He gets it all from his mother. I swear to God."

"Margaret is a good woman," Chuck answered with a laugh. "All I know, though, is that my Richard is a better man when he's around your son. I wish my older boy had had a friend like Thomas."

"Thanks, Chuck."

The crowd pushed through, and the pressing of the flesh swept the state representative away. John saw Kathleen running around and went to collect her and his wife, who was talking with Joan McGee and Anne Martin.

Thomas and Richard were talking as the class valedictorian, William Donohue, arrived and wished them both well in a most proper manner. It had been Dr. Diaz's last act as principal to deny Thomas the title, but Thomas could not be happier for William and congratulated him on getting accepted to the School of Engineering at the University of Illinois, Champaign. Richard left with William to go find the Donohue family, particularly Susan.

Thomas looked around for his family as the festivities were winding down. A large number of people were still milling about, and the noise was becoming wearisome. It had been a long day.

"Thomas!" a voice called out from behind him. He would recognize that voice anywhere. Marie made her way through a wall of people, came up to Thomas, and almost squeezed the life out of him. He returned the hug in kind.

She whispered in his ear, "That was a long, hard year, Thomas."

"But we made it through . . . together."

"I don't think I would have made it without you, Thomas," Marie confessed while giving him another bone-crushing hug.

"I know for a fact that I could not have made it without you, Marie. After all this, four years at St. Aloysius University should be a walk in the park." Thomas had accepted a full scholarship there, while Marie was offered a half scholarship. Alumni grants, courtesy of Mr. Charles McGee, would make up the rest of her tuition.

Thomas looked into her beautiful, smiling green eyes, the window to her even more beautiful soul. Eventually, through the bonds of holy matrimony, her soul and his would become one, united with each other and with eternal love and truth in a manner that could not be described with words. Only death would ever separate them. His most temperate smile gave no indication of the true joy, peace, freedom, and love erupting in his heart. He took Marie by the hand, leaving the past behind, and they walked off to face whatever tomorrow held, together forever.